TO DECEIVE A HIGHLANDER

THE SUTHERLANDS OF DORNOCH CASTLE ~ BOOK 1

CALLIE HUTTON

Copyright © 2022 by Callie Hutton

All rights reserved.

No part of this book may be reproduced in any form or by any electronic or mechanical means, including information storage and retrieval systems, without written permission from the author, except for the use of brief quotations in a book review.

ABOUT THE BOOK

Enemies to Lovers: He married the wrong sister.....or did he?

Laird Haydon Sutherland has made up his mind. 'Tis time to marry and he has offered marriage to Lady Elsbeth Johnstone, a quiet, demure lass who will never cause him a day of worry.

Lady Ainslee Johnstone, Elsbeth's feisty, stubborn twin will not allow the marriage to take place. The arrogant, fierce Sutherland will destroy her sweet sister, so they switch places on the wedding day.

Let the battles begin...

1

Just over the Scottish Lowlands border
Late Winter, 1653

"Nay, Da, I will not stand next to my sister and have some barbarian look us over as if we are horses to be sold." Lady Ainslee Johnstone crossed her arms over her chest and glared at her father.

Her da, Laird of Clan Johnstone of Lochwood Tower, waved the missive he held in his hand. "Ye will do as I tell ye, and that is the end of the discussion. I told ye it would be soon. I just received a missive that the Sutherland is arriving in a few days, and he intends to leave here with a betrothal." He pointed his finger in his two daughters' faces. "And leave here with a betrothal he will! 'Tis time for ye both to find husbands and get out from under me feet."

"Is he to take the two of us to wife, then?" Ainslee smirked and ignored her sister, Elsbeth's nudge.

'Twas always hard for her to hold her tongue, and

Elsbeth was ever the one who reminded her when she'd said too much. Ainslee hadn't learned over the years just how far her da could be pushed, so her sister's painful reminder told her now 'twas best to keep her mouth closed.

"I'll no' be taking sass from ye, lassie. Now be off with ye. I expect ye both to present yerselves in a gentle manner, and no' be shaming the Johnstone name." He gestured toward the staircase leading up to the bedchambers. "Go prepare yerselves to meet the laird. I expect ye to give him a warm welcome with decent meals and well-prepared bedchambers."

Arm-in-arm, the sisters left their father to his ale and headed to the bedchamber they shared. Although there was plenty of room in the castle for them to have their own chambers, they'd chosen to share their space since they'd quit the nursery.

Once they reached their bedchamber, Ainslee flopped on the bed and regarded her identical twin sister. At twenty years, they had ne'er spent more than several hours apart their entire lives. Even that was hard on them since Mam had insisted they sleep apart when at six years Ainslee had suffered a lung disease. Elsbeth had cried so hard Mam had to let her sleep on a pallet on the floor until Ainslee recovered.

"What say ye about this Sutherland Laird?" Ainslee shifted onto her side and propped up her head on her raised hand. "I'm sure he's a brute, and I canna imagine one of us married and living away from Lochwood Tower."

Elsbeth blew out a deep breath and sat next to her sister on the bed. "'Tis what troubles me. The few people I spoke to about the mon paint a picture of a large, loud, overbearing sort." She began to nibble on her fingernail until Ainslee slapped her hand away. "Stop."

Elsbeth considered her sister with tears in her eyes. "I doona want either of us to marry him."

Ainslee grasped her hand. "Aye. I agree. I had always hoped Da would let us marry someone here, so we could stay together."

"Ye ken that would ne'er happen. Marriages for lairds' daughters are made for alliances. The Sutherland is a powerful man, and I'm sure Da is honored to have the laird casting his eyes in our direction."

"Pfft! 'Tis tired I am of hearing about the honor of his attendance." Ainslee rose and walked to the window, smiling at the vision that greeted her. Even though the sky was gray, she loved the sight of Clan Johnstone lands. Hills rose and fell as far as she could see, with small cottages and robust farms dotting the land, carts rumbling over the drawbridge full of crofters and merchants with an abundance of goods ready to sell for the day. She glanced to the other side of the keep. Men's swords clashing in the lists, training. Always training.

She turned back and leaned against the window. "If we make ourselves as unappealing as possible, perhaps The Sutherland will decide he doesn't want one of us for a bride after all."

"Ainslee, ye heard Da. If we do anything to disgrace him, 'twill no' go well for us." Elsbeth drew circles on the bed cover with her fingernail. "I hear the Sutherland is quite good to look at."

"Ach! And as an overbearing, arrogant blicker, 'tis sure

I am he will want his wife to fall all o'er herself at his looks and bow to his every command."

"He is the Laird of Sutherland and both the law and the Church, say what we must do. Bow to his command, that is."

"No' for me. I will bow to no mon." Ainslee stabbed her chest with her thumb. "When I wed, I intend to be a partner, no' a submissive, cowering wife."

Elsbeth smiled at her sister. "As much as I doona want to marry the laird, I hope he passes over ye, or I fear there will be trouble."

DESPITE THE BRAVE words to her sister, Ainslee fought the knots in her stomach when Da sent for her and Elsbeth three days after his announcement of the imminent arrival of the Sutherland. The mon and his contingent had arrived and awaited her and Elsbeth in the great hall.

Earlier, she'd watched from the window as the group rode across the drawbridge, ten riders bearing The Sutherland clan's banner. It had not been difficult to pick out the Sutherland himself. Riding straight-backed in the saddle, he sat at least half a foot above the rest of the men, except for one other who almost reached his height.

Arrogance radiated from every pore in his body. He held his head high and stared straight ahead. She shivered and pulled back from the window, afraid he would look up and spot her staring at him like some lovesick fool.

"Ainslee, are you ready? Da will be stomping up here to drag us down soon." Elsbeth paced, her hands clenched together, her face pale. She stopped and placed her hands on her belly. "I worry that I will disgrace us all by emptying my stomach at the mon's feet."

"Calm yerself, sister. 'Tis only a mon." Her words didn't provide any more comfort to herself than they did her sister, from the look on the poor girl's face.

"Aye, a mon who Da promised will leave here with a betrothal."

Ainslee moved to the looking glass Da had brought back from his trip to London a few years before. The image of a pretty lass looked back. Her teeth were white and straight, her cheeks rosy, her eyes a deep green in a heart-shaped face. She had her mam's dark red, curly hair and pure white skin. 'Twas too bad she wasn't hunch-backed, with a mole on her nose, and whiskers on her chin.

She backed up and took a deep breath. "Let us go meet this laird who thinks to separate us." Ainslee wrapped her arm around Elsbeth's waist and together, as they'd been since before birth, they walked down the stone steps to their doom.

All the men stood as she and Elsbeth entered the great hall. They both hesitated as they took in the Sutherland men. Tall, broad, powerful. Not one of them was shorter than Da, who Ainslee thought was the tallest mon in the world.

"Come, come, lasses." Da waved at them from across the hall. Two men who resembled each other enough to be brothers stood on either side of him. Both men studied them carefully.

So, this is the time we are to be looked over as if we were horses to be sold. Should I open my mouth so he can inspect my teeth?

The one she was certain was the laird stared at her feet as his eyes made his way up her body until she had the urge to stick out her tongue when he got to her face. "'Tis it pleasin' to you, Laird? Do I have enough limbs to suit ye?"

Da sucked in a breath, closed his eyes, and shook his head. Ainslee expected the Sutherland to either storm from the hall or bellow at the top of his lungs. Instead, the demented mon roared with laughter. "Ye must be the feisty twin."

Not happy at being laughed at, Ainslee crossed her arms under her breasts. Once she saw the laird's eyes light up as he studied the rise of her flesh above her neckline, she dropped her arms. Randy oaf!

Da stepped closer to her and Elsbeth. "Laird, may I present to you my daughters, Lady Ainslee Johnstone and Lady Elsbeth Johnstone. Lasses, this is the Earl of Sutherland, Laird Haydon Sutherland of Clan Sutherland, who has honored us with his presence."

Ainslee didn't need to look at Da to know anger flashed in his eyes. She felt the tension radiating from him and would have to do some soothing to calm him. Both she and Elsbeth dipped a curtsy. "Welcome, Laird," they said in unison. Elsbeth offered a warm smile. Ainslee wanted to pinch her.

The Sutherland turned to the mon next to him. "May I present my brother, Conall Sutherland."

The brother seemed much more pleasant than the laird. He smiled at them, and although he also eyed them up and down, his eyes held a bit of mirth. "'Tis a pleasure to make the acquaintance of such lovely lasses. 'Tis hard to tell ye apart."

As Elsbeth generally became tongue-tied when speaking with anyone she hadn't known for years, Ainslee swallowed the lump of anger in her throat and offered a tight smile to the laird. "May I offer refreshments to you and your men, Laird?"

"Aye. That would be fine, lass."

She grabbed Elsbeth's hand. "Come, sister, let us seek refreshments for *The Sutherland* and his men."

Once they were out of earshot, Elsbeth turned on Ainslee. "You should not have said that about yer limbs. Da is angrier than I have ever seen him."

Ainslee sighed. "I know. It just came out without even thinking about it." She dragged her farther from the great hall. "Did you see the way he was staring at us? It was humiliating. I felt like a swine at the marketplace. I kept waiting for him to squeeze my arm to see if there was enough flesh on it."

"Nay. I dinna notice because I ne'er looked in his eyes. I find him too frightening. I've ne'er seen a mon so big. He's like a giant." Elsbeth shuddered.

"Aye, a pompous giant. 'Twas obvious from the man's demeanor that he thought much of himself."

They entered the kitchen, drawn to the smell of fresh bread and Cook's famous scones. "I doona think a few scones will satisfy the beast. Ye better send out a whole suckling."

"I saw the size of the mon. This will hold them until supper." Cook shoved a tray at Ainslee loaded with scones, bread, fresh butter, cheese, cold meat, and fruit.

"Ye should have sent for one of the kitchen maids to bring it to ye, since yer job is to catch the eye of the laird." Cook's belly shook with laughter.

Ainslee scowled and stomped out of the kitchen. Elsbeth ran to keep up with her. "Slow down, I can hardly catch up to you."

She turned to Elsbeth. "I have to move fast. This tray is blasted heavy." She turned back and ran smack into a wall. A warm, muscular wall. The tray slammed into the laird's belly, but he never uttered a sound. He must have been made of iron.

Once she recovered herself, she scowled at him. "What are ye doing here?"

His brows rose at her tone. "I came to help." He grabbed the tray from her hands. "Ye shouldn't be carrying this. Where are yer servants?"

Ainslee raised her chin. "I can carry a tray without assistance, Laird." She refused to use the term 'my laird' because he wasn't, and he would never be if she had anything to say about it.

One raised eyebrow this time was his only response. How did he do that? He turned and strode away from them, his long legs eating up the distance to the great hall. They would need to run as if in a race to catch up with him.

"Ye and the laird doona seem to get along verra well." Elsbeth stood with Ainslee as they watched the mon disappear into the great hall.

"Aye. Which means he'll cast his eye in yer direction. Ye must do something to turn him away from ye as well. Then he can go plague some other clan with his annoying presence and search for a wife."

They began their walk back to the great hall. "Why do ye dislike him so? I've ne'er seen you so annoyed with a mon. You usually have the lads all falling at yer feet, even with yer feisty ways."

Ainslee sighed. "I doona ken. He just brings shivers to me and makes me angry with his arrogant way."

It confused her, also, why the mon riled her. The resentment that his visit might separate her and Elsbeth for the first time in their lives was surely there, but something else, as well. He was certainly a handsome mon. His muscles matched his height, his shoulders so vast he blocked out the entire path to the great hall when she stood in front of him. His presence swamped her, urging her to step back to take in a full breath.

The laird's deep blue eyes seemed to bore right into her, as if he could read her thoughts. Wavy black-as-night hair loose on his shoulders, a broad forehead, firm jaw, and full lips would make most lasses swoon. Not her. Not ever her. Her job was to drive the mon away to leave them in peace.

With determined steps, they joined the men in the great hall.

"Ah, here they are." Da glared at the two of them.

Ainslee and Elsbeth took seats. Ainslee placed her hands on her lap, took on a demure manner and cast her eyes down. 'Twas easier to stay out of trouble if she dinna have to look at the mon.

"Lass, how many summers have ye seen?" The laird's smooth, deep voice rolled over her like warm honey. The shivers returned. Ainslee ignored the question, since Elsbeth could answer that.

When the silence grew, Elsbeth poked Ainslee in the ribs with her elbow.

"Ouch!" She glared at her sister.

"The laird asked you a question," Elsbeth whispered.

"You can answer for both of us," she whispered back.

Da's loud cough brought a sigh to Ainslee. Why was the mon picking on her? Surely, he would ne'er consider her for a bride. She raised her chin and stared the arrogant mon in the face. "My sister and I have seen twenty summers."

More annoying that his presence was his grin. The dratted mon was enjoying vexing her.

Conall finally spoke, breaking the tension. "I believe after that excellent repast, my brother and I would welcome a tour of yer fine keep, Laird." He gulped the rest of his ale and set the cup on the table.

"Aye, 'tis a wonderful idea. Daughters, I would ye accompany us on our tour." Da smiled warmly, but Ainslee saw the command in his eyes and inwardly groaned.

"Aye, Da."

The five of them rose and headed out the main door, Laird Sutherland walking between Da and Conall, with Elsbeth and Ainslee following, their arms linked.

As soon as they hit the air, Da began his discourse on all the wondrous parts of the castle. As he pointed out various buildings, her spirits immediately lifted with the sight of the crofters and merchants selling goods. From when she'd been a small girl, she loved wandering the bailey, deeply inhaling the enticing smell of the meat pies, scones, and oatcakes the bakers sold.

She had always been drawn to the tinkers who offered skeins of wool thread. There were several who rotated during the year. They purchased spun wool from other villages and sold it at the keeps they visited. Sometimes they offered herbs that did not grow in their gardens and were generally hard to find in the Lowlands.

Ainslee wandered from their group and stopped at a crofter the keep saw a few times a year. She fingered a lovely piece of lace that would look wonderful on one of her gowns. Engrossed in viewing the various patterns the crofter had, she stiffened when the hairs on the back of her neck stood up.

She didn't need to turn to know The Laird of Sutherland stood behind her. "Ah, here ye are lass. I thought we lost ye."

2

Haydon grinned at the lass's scowl as she finally turned. Why he enjoyed irritating her so much was a puzzle. From the first, it was obvious he would not take this one to wife. She was too outspoken, feisty, and they would ne'er suit. He wanted a peaceful life, and wee Elsbeth seemed the perfect woman to fit that role.

Despite having already made up his mind, he could certainly have a bit of fun at the lass's expense while they visited. Mayhaps his annoyance stemmed from his bewilderment. The lasses looked exactly alike, yet he felt no pull toward Elsbeth, and much too much of a draw toward her shrew of a sister.

That was another point in Elsbeth's favor. He had no time or desire to fall in love with a wife. Strong emotions could cripple a mon and make him vulnerable. There was no place in his life for the feisty sister whose passion could edge him toward something he had no intention of allowing.

However, while Elsbeth had a soft, demure look about her, and an easy demeanor, 'twas Ainslee's curvy body he imagined running his hands over in the marriage bed. She was the one he pictured screaming his name with pleasure as he plunged his staff into her soft moistness. A ridiculous notion since they'd only been acquainted for a few hours. Which why 'twas best to stay as far from the lass as possible and wind up the visit quickly, with a betrothal agreement between him and Lady Elsbeth.

"Is there something I can help you with, Laird? Surely you doona think I would get lost in my own bailey?" Her strained voice and tight smile brought him back to himself. Her annoyance warmed his heart.

"Nay. 'Tis sure I am yer quite able to take care of yerself."

"Indeed." She dropped the piece of lace she'd been fingering, and tucking her skirts against her legs, lest she touch his trews, she swept past him.

Haydon watched her hurry away and turned to the crofter. "How much for that wee bit of lace the lass was looking at?"

The mon related the price, and Haydon fished in the sporran that hung over his shoulder and withdrew two coins. As he held them out to the man, he said, "Ye better make that two pieces of lace."

He joined Conall, the Johnstone, and the two lasses, waiting in a circle for his return. Johnstone was pointing out something to Conall. Haydon handed the lace to the lasses. "'Tis sorry I am that I drove ye away from the crofter."

Elsbeth dipped a slight curtsy and lowered her eyes, a blush stealing up her cheeks. "Thank you, Laird."

Ainslee greeted him with raised eyebrows. "'Twas not necessary. I have my own coin."

"Ainslee!" Another nudge from her sister.

Ainslee sighed. "But thank ye."

Haydon held in his chuckle, and they continued with the tour.

Everywhere they went, clan members greeted the laird with ease, yet respect. 'Twas nice to know his future wife grew up in such pleasant surroundings. The Johnstone daughters had verra little to say while they strolled along. Most likely Elsbeth because she was shy and uncomfortable with strangers, and no doubt Ainslee was merely annoyed that she had to accompany them.

He'd been satisfied with Lochwood Tower thus far. The sound of swords clashing had drawn him to the lists to observe the men training. They appeared adept and worked hard under the supervision of two older men, who shouted orders and corrections to the men.

The tour took up another hour before Johnstone slapped him on the back as they returned from their visit to the impressive stables housing dozens of well fed and well-muscled beasts. "I think a large ale would do just fine right about now."

They all agreed and trooped back to the great hall.

"Da, please excuse us. We have much to do to prepare for tonight's feast." Ainslee spoke sweetly for the first time since he'd met her. Haydon couldn't help but think she was trying to appease her da who had seemed annoyed with her since their introduction earlier.

"Aye, see that all is well, lass."

The lasses scurried away, and the three men settled at

a table. A serving wench carried in mugs and a pitcher of ale.

"Ye've a good, solid keep here, Laird." Haydon took a sip, the cool refreshing liquid sliding down his throat, easing the dryness from their walk. "Yer men seem ready to do battle."

"Thank ye." Johnstone leaned forward. "What do ye hear about the rebellion, Laird? Being so far south from the noise up north, we doona hear much here in Kintyre."

"Our messengers tell me William Cunningham is sending word to all the clans, hoping to rally them to support the rebellion. I've had word from Cunningham's camp that they are looking at our own Dornoch Castle for a gathering place."

"Since yer considering taking one of my lasses to wife, 'tis hopeful I am that ye are well prepared to defend yer castle."

Ordinarily Haydon would be insulted at such words, but since he'd never fathered a bairn, 'twas hard to take offense at the mon's question. "Aye, we are well protected. Our men train for hours daily. I doubt there will be any fighting near Dornoch, just a place for Cunningham to rally the clans."

The Scott nodded. "We're ready to join the rebellion. See that ye send word when the time comes. The hour has arrived to get rid of the Sassenach and leave the clans to deal with their own, like we've been doing for years."

Haydon raised his mug of ale. *"Slàinte!"*

"Slàinte!" Conall and Johnstone responded.

A mon wearing the colors of the Johnstone clan entered the hall. "Laird, ye are needed in the bailey. A skirmish has erupted between two crofters, and they request yer presence to settle the matter."

Johnstone stood and addressed Haydon and Conall. "If ye will excuse me, I will see to this problem."

Haydon waved off the mon. "'Tis fine. I would like to take a turn at some of yer men in the lists. No' a good idea for a mon to stay too long from his sword."

As Haydon and Conall made the walk from the great hall to the lists, several lasses turned their heads to study them, smiling and swishing their hips. Since he was here to contract a marriage with one of the laird's daughters, he would not disrespect them by encouraging any of the wenches.

Conall, however, always with the charm and natural attraction to the lasses stopped and flirted with one or two until Haydon grew restless and reminded him where they were headed.

"Ye need a lass in yer bed, brother. I've told you that many times before," Conall groused as he caught up to Haydon.

"Aye, and that is what this trip is all about. I won't be casting any looks at the lasses here with plans to return home with a betrothal."

The time had come to do his duty and find a wife and get a few bairns on her. Conall was his heir right now, but he wanted sons of his own. Strong lads and bonny wee lasses. The keep would run smoother with a wife, also. After *Mamaidh* had passed away, he'd expected his sister, Donella, of fifteen years to take over the keep duties. However, *Mamaidh* had often referred to Donella as a 'dreamer.'

The lass had a hard time organizing and supervising

the servants. When he pointed out to her a tear in his shirt, or the rushes that needing changing, or the kitchen garden that was growing wild, she would smile and promise to see to it, and then disappear.

A wife would solve a lot of those problems, and wee Elsbeth would do just fine. He had no desire for a great passion or love. That was for women to stew about. A good romp in his bed, bairns to follow, hot meals on the table, and a well-run keep. That was all he needed from a wife.

Clashing of swords, grunts, and shouts from the men greeted them as they turned the corner of the keep. They stood and studied the men for a few minutes. One of the lads they'd seen during their tour walked up to them. "So are ye ready to take on a few of us, Sutherland?"

"Aye, but are yer men ready to take us on?" He grinned and slid his sword from the scabbard strapped to his back. He shrugged out of his shirt and tossed it on a stone bench, leaving him in trews and boots. Conall followed, and the brothers entered the fray.

It felt good to have his sword in his hand again, in the middle of a list, parrying with Johnstone's men. For the most part, they were skilled, but Haydon took pride in the fact that any one of his men could take down most of Johnstone's warriors.

"Sutherland!" A mon strode up to him. Perhaps an inch or two shorter than him, the warrior was braw, with a mustache and beard covering everything on his face except his eyes. Stringy hair to his mid back was held behind his head with a leather strap.

Haydon wiped the sweat from his forehead with his arm. "Aye."

The warrior stood with his hands on his hips, legs spread, and a huge grin on his face. "'Tis time to take on a real mon if yer no' afraid."

Haydon spit on the ground. "Afraid? Ne'er."

"Stand back!" The mon waved his massive arms, and all those in the lists stopped and gathered at the edge, forming a circle.

Haydon believed he was being challenged not just to prove his worth on the battlefield, but as a husband to one of the Johnstone lasses. 'Twas a test he was up for. He wiped his sweaty palm on his trews and took a firmer grip on his sword.

The two men bent forward, then circled each other until Haydon saw an opening and swung. Swords clashed as they came forward, and then withdrew. After three more parries, Haydon identified a weakness in the mon, but for the purposes of a show he wouldn't employ the tactics to disarm him yet.

Each time the warrior lunged forward forcing Haydon to jump back, cheers erupted from the crowd. Shouts of encouragement drew clansmen and women from their duties to join the circle of men.

Christ's toes, it felt good to be truly challenged. Most times 'twas only his brother who could make him sweat. After about ten minutes of playing with the mon, Haydon feigned left, then right, then snapped his sword underneath his opponent's, the weapon flying from his hand into the air as his feet slipped out from under him and he tumbled to the ground on his arse.

Haydon placed the tip of his sword to the man's throat. Both men breathed heavily, their panting the only sound, as the crowd grew silent. Surely, they did not think he would kill the mon? 'Twas certainly not the way to win the hand of the laird's daughter. "Good fight, mon." He pulled his sword back and reached out to help the warrior to his feet.

Backslapping and congratulations followed. Haydon shook the sweat from his forehead, his eyes traveling up the side of the keep. At a window above, one of the Johnstone lasses stood, watching the display. Uncertain which one it was, he bowed and offered a smile. When a scowl appeared on her face, he laughed out loud, kenning 'twas Ainslee who had watched him defeat their best warrior.

AFTER A BATH, when he had to gently reject the wench sent to help him bathe from offering any other services without hurting the lass's feelings, Haydon joined the Johnstone in the mon's solar.

A room made for comfort and status, it included a fireplace and decorative woodwork as well as tapestries on every wall. An adjoining room appeared to be for a lady's use with the walls painted green with gold stars.

"Ye wished to see me, Laird?" Haydon settled in the comfortable chair next to the Johnstone, in front of the low-burning fireplace.

"Aye. 'Tis only a day ye've been here, but already stories have reached my ears about yer prowess on the lists and how you defeated my cousin, Bryan."

"Yer cousin is a fine mon and a skilled warrior." Haydon grinned. "I am just a tad better, is all."

The Johnstone laughed. "And ye have a sense of humor." He stood and poured two mugs of ale from a pitcher on the table behind them. He handed one to Haydon and raised his glass. *"Slainte."*

"Slainte." Haydon responded, and they both took hardy gulps of the refreshing drink.

"Ye've seen my two lasses." He shook his head and settled back into his chair. "I'm afraid my Ainslee is a bit outspoken, a trait her mam and I tried to halt, but 'tis just something in the lass that she can't control."

"Everyone can control what they say." Haydon sat back further in the chair and rested his booted foot on his knee. "The lass just needs a firmer hand. I'm thinking as her da, you have too much of a soft spot for the lass."

The Johnstone nodded and sighed. "I think yer right." His eyes sparkled as he leaned forward and regarded Haydon. "Perhaps a stern husband is the best thing for the lass. Ye seem staunch enough."

Haydon hadn't intended to make his choice known so soon, but it was best to get the dangerous idea out of the laird's mind about to which lass he would be offering a proposal. Attempting to tame the termagant would take away precious hours from his duties as laird.

He shifted in his seat as the thought of directing all that passion to where it would bring them the most pleasure had his staff swelling with the vision. Best to get that picture out of his mind, as well.

"I hadn't planned on making a choice so soon, but I'm leaning toward wee Elsbeth."

The laird's shoulders slumped, and he drank the last of his ale. "'Tis sorry I will be to see the lass leave me, but I kenned 'twould happen one day." He stiffened in his chair and nodded his approval. "A good decision, laird. Elsbeth will be obedient and caring for ye and any bairns ye give her. She is skilled in household management, gardening, and medicaments for yer clan."

"Excellent." Haydon smiled, happy with his choice. Perhaps time away from her twin, the obvious dominant one, might make the lass stronger. Since he was not one to wander from bed to bed, especially when married, he would use his skill in the bedchamber to bring passion to their bed sport.

He shoved away the vision of the other lass's fire and spirit he'd already seen in other ways. Ah, there was a lass who would keep a mon from his duties just to spend time discovering new ways to make the lass scream with pleasure.

"So as not to extend the concern over who will be leaving us, with yer permission, I'd like to call the lasses in to tell them of yer decision. 'Twill make the leaving easier I believe if they have time together to prepare."

Haydon nodded, and the laird headed toward the door, then turned. "I doona suppose ye have another mon about yer place who would take on the other one? Yer brother, perhaps?"

Thinking of Conall and the many lasses he had offering him a tumble, he smiled. "Nay. I doona think that would work."

"Aye."

The lasses' bedchamber must not have been far from the solar, since the Johnstone returned within minutes. Or else they had been waiting outside, expecting the laird's question.

As usual, wee Elsbeth walked in with her head down, her fingers clasped in front of her. Ainslee marched alongside her, her defiant chin raised, matching him stare for stare. He had to bite the inside of his cheek to keep from smiling. Ah, but the lass was dangerous. 'Twas a good thing she would be left behind when his bride arrived at Dornoch.

Once they were all settled in their seats, the Johnstone addressed the lasses. "My dear daughters, the laird has made up his mind who he wishes to take to wife."

Both lasses stiffened, and Elsbeth's face grew quite pale, her interlaced fingers turning white, her eyes still downcast.

"The Earl of Sutherland, Laird Haydon Sutherland of Dornoch Castle, has decided to offer his hand in marriage, forming an alliance between the Sutherlands and the Johnstones, to my lovely daughter, Elsbeth."

Ainslee narrowed her eyes at Haydon just as wee Elsbeth let out a sigh and slid from her chair to the floor in a dead faint.

3

"Doona just stand there, help her!" Ainslee snapped at the Sutherland and Da as she dropped to her knees and took Elsbeth's hand. Both men stared down at her sister as if they'd ne'er seen her before.

"Aye, I'm thinking the joyful excitement has gotten to her." Da looked around as if someone would magically appear to help him out of the dilemma.

"Stand aside, lass. I'll carry her to her bedchamber." The laird bent to one knee, and before Ainslee could protest, he scooped Elsbeth up in his arms and stood. "Show me the way."

Joyful excitement, indeed. Elsbeth had fainted when she simply imagined life with the arrogant laird who picked her up with such ease and carried her like she weighed no more than a bag of feathers.

"'Tis not proper for ye to be carrying my sister to her bed, but 'tis this way." Ainslee hurried from the room and down the corridor to their chamber. Elsbeth was more prone to swoons than Ainslee had ever been, and certainly the shock of Da's announcement was more than the poor lass could stand.

The sound of the laird's boots on the stone floor echoed behind her as they strode down the corridor until they reached their bedchamber. Without an invitation, the laird barreled through the door and deposited Elsbeth on the bed.

The bedchamber she and Elsbeth had shared for years was a large one, with an attached solar. Now, however, the room seemed smaller, as if it had shrunk overnight. The laird took up all the room and all the air. Which was precisely why Ainslee was having a problem accessing some for her lungs. She stiffened her shoulders and raised her chin. "If you will excuse us, Laird, I will attend my sister."

"Will she be all right? Does she do this often?"

Ainslee stepped back from the mon who was entirely too close and whose verra presence rattled her so. Her eyes snapped with barely controlled anger. "Are ye afraid ye might have just offered to take to wife an unsound woman? Is that yer concern? Are ye sorry in yer choice?"

Ainslee could almost see the steam come from the mon's ears. "'Twas not my worry at all. I am merely concerned for the lass's welfare. As for being the wrong choice, the only other one is ye, and if that was forced upon me, 'twould be more than swooning I would do. A head-first tumble from the window beyond would be a happier fate."

She fisted her hands at her side and gritted her teeth. "If ye will excuse me, *Laird*, I would attend my sister now.

There is no further need for ye." In an inexcusable show of rudeness, she turned her back and bent over Elsbeth.

Only after she heard his footsteps stomping off, did her knees give way and she sat alongside Elsbeth, taking a deep breath. Her heart pounded, and her stomach felt as though a nest of honeybees swarmed inside. Ach, how she despised the mon. And to think sweet, demure Elsbeth would be married to the lout!

She pushed the hair back from Elsbeth's forehead. "My poor sister. What did ye ever do to deserve such a fate?"

'TWAS THE LAST day of the Sutherlands' visit. Ainslee was only too glad to see them go, but her heart ached for her sister. Elsbeth had retreated into herself from the time she'd awoken from her swoon until the supper they now sat at, awaiting Da's announcement of the betrothal. It had been decided due to the possibility of a rebellion in the near future, the wedding would take place in a fortnight.

The Sutherland men would return to Dornoch Castle on the morrow to prepare for the wedding, and the bride, accompanied by her father and sister and a troop of Johnstone warriors, would set out in a sennight.

Ainslee had tried over the past few days to calm her sister, but she was afraid her dislike of the mon was coming through in her attempts to make it all seem pleasant.

"'Twill no' be so bad, Elsbeth. Ye will have yer own household to manage. From what Da told us, the Sutherland Clan is large and wealthy. And one day ye will have bairns to love."

That, perhaps, had not been the best idea to put into Elsbeth's head since she paled at the thought of what the appearance of bairns would require.

If Ainslee were true to herself, she would admit the thought of climbing into bed with the Sutherland would be the only reward a woman would have for wedding the arrogant mon. She had spent the rest of their visit forcing herself to stop watching when he took a turn at the lists each day. Especially since he was apt to remove his shirt and fight in just a tartan or trews and boots. And of course, the blasted mon always managed to catch her watching—grinning at her, no less.

Ach, but the mon had muscles. Hard as stone, they rippled as he swung his sword. He tied his hair back from his face, but always a strand would fall forward, teasing his hard jaw. He focused entirely on his opponent with an intensity that had her stomach fluttering, wondering what it would be like to have that passion directed at a woman.

Not her, of course. But a small part of her that she refused to acknowledge envied her sister that part of her life. Nothing else, of course. The mon was an arrogant, overbearing oaf and would probably spend his days directing her sister's life.

She'd known from a mere child that marriage for her would not involve submitting to some mon, flattering his overblown ego, and no' having a say in how she conducted her life. Unfortunately, 'twas not the way things were for women, but she'd intended to chase away any mon who descended upon them to offer marriage if she didn't feel as though she would be happy.

Ach, and the worse would be if she fell in love with the

mon she married. Then she would have no peace at all, happily deferring to him in all things. Nay, not for her.

Now she sat at table alongside Conall Sutherland, who she'd found over their visit to be a verra pleasant mon. He flirted with her, but he flirted with all the lasses. Ainslee had spent far too much time steering serving wenches and scullery maids back to their duties instead of trying to gain Conall's attention.

"Yer sister is a charming young lass. I believe, after a while, she will be happy with my brother." Conall spoke to Ainslee as he sipped from his mug and stared at Elsbeth.

Elsbeth had grown more subdued and anxious since the announcement. The past three nights Ainslee had awakened to her sister pacing the floor in their room. When she attempted to calm her, Elsbeth brushed her off, telling her 'twas nothing to be done for her. She was doomed.

"I wish I could be certain of that." She leaned in close to Conall and lowered her voice. "I doona mean to offend ye, but I find yer brother arrogant, barbaric, and highhanded."

Conall burst out laughing, drawing the attention of others on the dais. "Lass, please doona hold back. Tell me what ye really think of the mon."

Ainslee's face flushed, and she caught Da looking at her curiously and the Sutherland glowering in her direction. Dinna the mon ever smile?

Aye, he did. When he caught her watching him swing a sword.

Attempting to regain her dignity, she raised her chin. "Perhaps I was a bit harsh, but I doona think he will do right by my sister. She is a shy lass, easily upset, and no' one to take too quickly to strangers." She studied Elsbeth as she nodded, her eyes downcast as the Sutherland lowered his head and spoke to her.

Suddenly, the thought of them being separated hit Ainslee with a force like when she'd been tossed from a horse as a young girl. All the breath left her body. Her hands shook as she reached for her mug of ale.

"Are ye all right, lass? Ye seem a bit upset of a sudden." Conall looked at her with concern.

Good glory, she was about to cry right here in front of everyone. "If you will excuse me." She went to stand and Conall stood with her. "I will escort you outside. Ye look as though ye need a bit of fresh air."

"No need," she muttered, but he followed her anyway.

Once outside, she felt a bit better. Conall ne'er said a word but walked with her as she took in the cool night air.

Attempting to get herself under control, she looked up at the sky. "How many stars do ye think are up there?"

"More than we can count." After a few minutes when she couldn't think of anything to say, Conall took her hand. "Doona worry so about yer sister. Ye will be welcome to stay at Dornoch Castle for as long as ye like to see her settled."

Ainslee shook her head. "Nay. Da is anxious to see me wed. Now that Elsbeth is settled, he'll be looking for a husband for me."

He patted her hand. "Doona fret. She will be fine."

Nay. She won't.

They started a slow walk back to the castle when an idea Ainslee hadn't been allowing herself to seriously consider pushed to the front of her mind. She could do it.

It would be a disaster at first, but she could handle anything, where Elsbeth could not.

Now all she had to do was convince her sister.

"Are you addlepated? We could ne'er get away with that. Da would be furious, and the laird could even beat ye!" Elsbeth regarded her with horror when Ainslee told her of her plan that night. They had just returned from supper, and the announcement had been made. Early the next morn, the Sutherland men would ride for home. Elsbeth was in possession of the betrothal ring, and all was set.

"Of course, we could get away with it. We look exactly alike. The Sutherland will never know the difference until 'tis too late."

"Aye, too late, but then what? God's bones, what might he do to ye?"

Ainslee raised her chin. "Whate'er it is, I can handle it."

"But you hate the mon!" Elsbeth paced again, wringing her hands. "I canna allow ye to do it. 'Tis not fair to ye."

"And 'tis fair ye doona get to marry someone you want to wed? Someone who doesn't make ye pace the floors in the middle of the night? If we do this, ye will be free to pick yer own husband."

"Nay. Da will find someone else. Maybe even worse."

"Hah! There is no worse. He will be so shocked by what we've done, it will take him a while to recover. Meanwhile, we will have time to convince Da to allow you to stay with me at Dornoch and maybe even find someone there. Doona forget the rebellion. There won't be a whole lot of time to go fishing for a husband. And 'twill probably be safer for you there, anyway. 'Tis a major holding the Sutherland has."

Elsbeth collapsed on the side of the bed. "What about ye? 'Tis of a life of misery ye will be facing."

"Pfft. Doona fash yerself. I can handle the Sutherland. He doesn't frighten me."

In fact, the idea of crossing verbal swords with him held great appeal. And there was the bedding…

She flushed as she thought of seeing all that golden skin and rippling muscles uncovered. Ach, but he would be so angry at being thwarted. That alone made her smile. She took Elsbeth's hand and gave her a curt nod. "Aye, we will do it."

BUSY WITH WEDDING preparations and packing all their belongings, the time between the Sutherland's departure and their arrival at Dornoch Castle passed quickly. Much too quickly, and in no time, it seemed the day of the wedding was upon them.

Ainslee and Elsbeth were in the bedchamber assigned to them at Dornoch. Ainslee wore the gown that had been sewn for the bride, and her sister wore the one meant for Ainslee.

They stared at each other, two women who looked exactly alike, except for the glow in Ainslee's eyes. She could do this. It would save her sister from a life of misery. She loved her twin far too much to let her suffer as she would surely do married to the Sutherland.

The betrothal ring given to her sister hung heavy on Ainslee's finger, and she fussed with it as she wondered at the uproar they were about to cause. There was nothing to be had for it, and she would no' change her mind. They had made sure to ply Da with whisky before they retired to the bedchamber to dress. Hopefully, he would be too much in his cups to realize they'd switched places.

Taking a deep breath, she picked up the sprig of pink heather laying on the bed, considered to be good luck to the bride and groom on their wedding day, and looked at Elsbeth. "Are we ready?"

"If yer sure?"

She gave her a curt nod. "Aye. I'm sure."

Ainslee kept her eyes downcast as the two of them walked with a slightly swaying Laird Johnstone the distance from the castle to the front of the small Kirk on the Sutherland grounds where they were to be married. Since the taking of the vows were traditionally spoken outside the Kirk, Elsbeth stopped about five feet from where the priest and the Sutherland stood.

Ainslee peeked from under her lashes as she continued to his side and sucked in a deep breath, all fear of her trickery vanishing at the sight of her future husband. Dressed in the full formal regalia of the Sutherland clan, the laird stood tall and proud as he awaited her. His wavy, black hair was pulled back and tied at the back of his head, with a few shorter strands already attempting to make their escape. His white linen shirt was tucked into the green, blue, white, and red pleated plaid of the Sutherland Clan, which came barely to his knees. The tartan thrown over his shoulder was anchored with the Sutherland Clan badge and a Cairngorm brooch.

A jewel-hilted sword hung at his side from a black patent leather sword belt, ornamented with buckles and more jewels. A soft, white, furry sporran covered the front of the plaid. His stockings needed no garters to hold them up, with the bulging muscles of his calves doing a fine job of it.

He was magnificent, everything about him large and powerful, and she was about to enrage the beast. Unable to help herself, she stopped and looked directly into his eyes.

A mistake.

He frowned and cocked his head in a questioning manner. Before he could say anything, she dropped her eyelids and moved alongside him.

After a moment, the laird leaned down. "Ye look lovely, lass."

Her mouth was so dry she could not respond, but merely nodded.

"Have you nothing to say?" Something in his voice sent shivers down her spine. A tinge of confusion, perhaps anger.

She shook her head, continuing to stare at her feet. She told herself 'twas not because she was fearful of the mon, but in keeping with her pretense of being the shy Elsbeth.

"Shall we begin?" The priest's voice sounded as if it came from a distance, and for a moment she was afraid she would faint.

No. I must be strong. This is for Elsbeth.

"Aye, let us begin." The Sutherland pried her left hand from the heather she grasped like a lifeline and took her hand in his. Hopefully, he would excuse her sweaty palm and shaking hand to mere bridal nerves.

The priest wrapped their hands together with the Sutherland plaid and began. During the preliminary rumbling about the sanctity of marriage by the priest, the laird leaned down again. "Are ye all right, lass? Ye seem a bit out of sorts today."

Oh, Lord, had he already guessed and was playing with her? If he knew, why didn't he bellow out the truth and disgrace them all?

"Nay. I am fine. Thank ye," she barely whispered. By now, her entire body shook, and if the priest did not get to the important part soon, she would run screaming back to the keep.

The priest cleared his throat. "My laird, please repeat after me: *I, Haydon Alasdair Michael Sutherland, Earl of Sutherland, Laird of Clan Sutherland of Dornoch, take thee—*" He paused and nodded at the laird.

"I, Haydon Alasdair Michael Sutherland, Earl of Sutherland, Laird of Clan Sutherland of Dornoch, take thee—" he stopped and squeezed Ainslee's hand. "Look at me lass."

Ainslee raised her eyes and whispered. "—Lady Ainslee Elizabeth Rose Johnstone,"

His lips tightened, and just as she thought he would stop the ceremony and demand she and Elsbeth switch places, he stared directly into her eyes and repeated "Lady Ainslee Elizabeth Rose Johnstone."

The priest looked back to his book and then to the two of them with a frown. "I doona understand."

"Continue," her groom snapped.

"Aye." The priest cleared his throat. *"To be my wedded wife, to have and to hold from this day forward, for better for worse, for richer for poorer, for fairer or fouler, in sickness and in health, to love and to cherish, till death us depart, according to God's holy ordinance; and thereunto I plight thee my troth."*

4

Haydon held his temper, and not wishing to disgrace *his wife*, or provoke her father, finished the ceremony, his curt responses causing Conall to stare at them both with confusion.

As they turned to face the gathered crowd, Haydon glared in Elsbeth's direction. Her eyes grew wide, and she clutched her throat.

Then the lass promptly fainted.

He tugged on Ainslee's arm as she moved to go to her sister. "Stay right where you are, lass."

"But my sister…"

"Aye, yer sister. The one who was supposed to be standing here next to me. Or did the two of you lose yer memories and forget who was to be the bride?"

To his astonishment, Ainslee's eyes filled with tears, and she whispered, "I'm so sorry. I was just concerned for my sister."

"So ye think I'm such a brute, then? Are ye sure ye can survive marriage to me? Or are ye to be the martyr sacrificed on the altar of sisterly love?" He moved them forward. "Yer sister looks fine, let us move along to the wedding feast."

Indeed, Elsbeth was now on her feet, looking everywhere except at him and Ainslee. Deep down inside, where thoughts he refused to acknowledge gathered, a small voice was congratulating him on the switch. Elsbeth was a sweet young lass, but it had bothered him a bit after he'd made his choice that she was no stronger than Donella. Lord knew the keep was falling apart under her guidance. Ainslee would be a much better choice to make things right.

But Lord help him. She would no' be easy to live with.

The great hall was overflowing with clansmen and guests from neighboring clans who Haydon counted among his allies. He escorted Ainslee to the dais where they took their seats to accept congratulations from a stream of well-wishers.

In between handshakes and lewd comments about the coming night, Haydon leaned close to his wife's ear. "Ye have a lot of explaining to do, *wife*. Doona think because I'm smiling like a fool that defying yer laird as ye did sits well with me."

The lass had the nerve to hitch her chin up. "Ye were no' my laird when my sister and I decided to switch."

His jaw muscles tightened. "Aye, and it's sure I am she had to be talked into it. By you."

Ainslee opened her mouth to speak just as her da stopped in front of them. "Ainslee?"

"Aye, Da."

The Johnstone glanced between the two of them. "I thought 'twas Elsbeth that was to be married today."

It was clear the mon had enjoyed more than a few ales along with the whisky as he stood in front of them swaying on his feet. Haydon looked over at Ainslee with raised brows. "Explain to yer da, *wife*."

She took a deep breath. "My laird changed his mind at the last minute." She looked at Haydon, her eyes pleading. No doubt the lass referred to him as *my laird* to encourage him to remain silent on the matter.

He had no more desire to embarrass her now than he had at the ceremony. Regardless of her manipulation, she was now his wife, and deserved his loyalty. After a few moments, he said, "'Tis true. After much consideration, I decided Lady Ainslee would suit better, and both yer daughters were willing to abide by my request."

Haydon doubted the mon understood him, since he continued to sway back and forth. "Glad it all turned out, Laird. Now I just have to worry about getting my other precious daughter married off."

"About that, Da," Ainslee jumped in. "I was hoping Elsbeth could stay with me for a while." She glanced sideways at Haydon. "To help me settle in."

It took all of Haydon's control not to burst out with laughter. He doubted his wife ever needed her sister's help to settle into anything. But if the lass wanted to keep Elsbeth nearby, that was fine with him.

His only thoughts at the time were getting through the meal and the following drinking and dancing so he could retire to his bedchamber with his wife. He might as well get the benefits of having married the wrong woman. Ainslee's spit and fire would be verra welcomed in his bed.

"Aye, if yer sister wants to stay with ye, 'tis no' a problem for me."

The Johnstone leaned forward, almost tumbling onto the table separating him and his daughter. "Ye must try to get the lass married."

"Aye, Da. I will try."

He stumbled off. Haydon and Ainslee grinned at each other. She shook her head. "He usually doesn't drink so much. I'm afeared he will have a huge headache come morning."

"Ye doona seem to be enjoying yer food, *wife*." Haydon nodded toward her almost-full trencher.

"Aye. 'Twould be the polite thing to say I've lost my appetite, but the truth of the matter is the food is not to my liking."

Haydon sighed. "'Tis true. That is one of the reasons I needed a wife. My sister, Donella, has been running things since *Mamaidh* died, and I don't think she's meant to do such a job. She's more herself when she's off doing things that seem silly to me but makes her happy."

"Ye are concerned with yer sister's happiness?"

Aye, it seemed the lass did see him as an unfeeling brute. "Does that surprise ye, lass? Yes, my wee sister's happiness is important to me. Mayhaps I am not the beast ye think me to be." He leaned in closer to whisper in her ear. "Could it be ye feel ye made a mistake by switching sisters? There are duties that would never fall to Donella that *my wife* will satisfy."

She drew in a deep breath, and a flush covered her face. He watched her over the rim of his ale cup, wondering if her reaction was from thinking of the time they would retire to his bedchamber?

He had to push those thoughts away himself. Imagining her mass of dark red hair spread over his pillow as he worshipped her body would only torture him until 'twas time to retire.

"Let the dancing begin!" Conall shouted from the middle of the floor. Tables were immediately shoved against the wall to make room. Dancing was a big part of a wedding feast, and there had been just enough ale to make even the least capable dancer hop around like a fool.

Conall strode over to them, his arms outstretched. "Come, Laird, ye and yer bonny wife must start the dancing with the Grand March."

The air rang with the fiddlers' few jarring notes, then went into a march. Ainslee and Haydon both stood. He took her hand and led her to the space recently cleared. He and Ainslee would march to the music from the fiddlers and the bagpipers. Elsbeth and Conall as the maid of honour and best mon would follow, with the guests behind them.

Once they circled the room, the music switched to a lively tune. Despite his size, Haydon was always a graceful dancer and enjoyed it. He pulled Ainslee into his arms, and they moved into the country dance. He was pleased when she followed him so easily, but being a Johnstone lass, she no doubt had been dancing since she could walk.

A few hours later, after another two dances in a row, he clasped her hand and led her back to the dais to recover. They downed glasses of ale as their breath returned.

"Ye are quite the dancer, my laird."

"Aye. I enjoy it almost as much as sword play." He leaned in close to her ear. "Or bed play."

He laughed out loud when her recently faded flush from dancing returned. Before he was able to comment on that, several of the ladies approached their table, their grins telling. "'Tis time for the bedding ceremony, my lady."

AINSLEE HAD BEEN successful since the morning pushing to the back of her mind what would happen once the celebrations had ended. Not that they were over since they would go on for hours, but the bedding ceremony was traditionally set during the festivities.

She was certainly not looking forward to it. It was humiliating, and she had no desire to have a bunch of drunk, lewd men drool over her and her new husband in bed.

She grabbed Haydon's shirt and pulled him close. "My laird, I must have a word with ye."

"Come, come, now dearie," one of the ladies said as she reached across the table and took Ainslee's hand. "We need to prepare ye for yer husband."

The ladies all burst out laughing, and she tried once more to speak with Haydon, but he was enjoying her distress. A bit too much to her mind.

"My laird." She reached her hand out, but he only continued to laugh. The arrogant oaf.

The ladies pulled her across the room to the sound of hoots and laughter from the guests. Up the stairs they went to what she assumed was the laird's bedchamber. A bath had been prepared, and within minutes, the women had her unclothed and sitting in warm, perfumed water.

She looked around frantically for Elsbeth, but she was

nowhere in sight. "Where is my sister?" she asked right before a bucket of water was dumped over her head.

With her stepmother dead when she was just a child, no one had spoken to her about her wedding night. Why hadn't she sought out one of the serving girls or maids who spent their time giggling about this?

It seemed within minutes she was dragged from the bathtub, dried, and wrapped in a linen. Amid more giggling and comments about what was to come, she relaxed as she sat before the fireplace while one of the women brushed her hair.

She was tempted to ask for some information or advice but decided their hilarity would only cause her more anxiety. It seemed the women had been enjoying their ale also.

Shortly, she was hauled across the room and slipped into bed wearing nothing. "Um, is there a nightdress I can wear? I brought some with me." She pointed to the trunk in the corner.

"No, my lady. 'Tis yer wedding night. No need for a nightdress. I'm sure the laird has been waiting for this for some time." One of the older women winked at her, and the others all laughed.

They hustled around the room, picking up her clothing and the wet linen. Just as she was beginning to relax and feel a bit sleepy, loud singing and stomping up the stairs brought her wide awake.

Her heart pounding, she pulled the coverlet up to her neck. The women continued to laugh and nudge each other.

The door burst open, and Haydon was shoved into the room from behind. About ten men, it seemed, shouted and laughed behind him. "Time for the bedding ceremony," one of the men shouted, waving his cup of ale that spilled on the floor.

Ainslee pulled the coverlet up farther until the only thing visible was her eyes and hair. She backed up against the headboard and tried verra hard to calm herself.

The crowd of both grinning men and women around her bed almost brought up the wee bit of food she had eaten. Surely, they weren't going to stand there and watch?

Haydon sat on the bed alongside her and retrieved her hand from the bedcovers. "Thank ye all for the escort upstairs, but I believe my wife and I would prefer some privacy."

She almost fell in love with him at that moment.

"Nay, laird. 'Tis a tradition." Shouts of 'nay' and 'tradition' echoed through the room. Haydon shook his head. "Nay, my friends."

"The church requires it," shouted one of the women. "The marriage must be consummated to make it legal."

"Ye can easily see my bonny wife. Do any of ye here believe I am incapable of doing such?" His brows rose, and Ainslee hid her giggle. She couldn't imagine who would look at Haydon with his muscles and definite appeal and believe he could not perform his duty.

He stood and made a shooing motion. "Off with ye now. I am yer laird, and I order it."

With a great deal of grumbling and moaning, the revelers shuffled out of the room, denied their moments of sport. Haydon followed and closed the door, turning the lock.

Ainslee breathed a sigh of relief. She cleared her verra dry throat. "Thank ye, my laird."

Haydon began to undress, shrugging his plaid off his shoulder and unbuttoning his liene, watching her the entire time.

She inhaled deeply, fascinated, as all that golden skin and hard muscles were uncovered. Once his shirt was gone, he began to loosen the pleats in his plaid, and then stopped. "Close yer mouth, lass."

Her eyes flew up to his face. The arrogant arse grinned at her. She shrugged and began to pick at the cover. "'Tis no matter to me."

"Aye. I can see that."

The rustle of clothing dropping to the floor had her heart pumping and muscles tightening. She studied her interlaced fingers as she felt the bed dip and the covers move as he settled alongside her.

The warmth from his—naked—body practically set her on fire. Dear God, what had she gotten herself into? She kenned marriage had been in her future from the time she drew her first breath. If it wasn't this handsome mon with all his appeal, it could be an auld, fragile one making a last attempt at a son.

"Look at me, Ainslee."

Taking a deep breath, she looked over at her husband.

Her husband.

The mon who had every right to her body, her person, and controlled her welfare. The law and the Church agreed. At the moment, it was hard for her to remember why she thought it had been a good idea to switch places with her sister.

Then she realized poor Elsbeth would have swooned

several times by now. Yes. She could take her sister's place alongside this mon. She raised her chin and looked him in the eye. "Aye, my laird?"

He reached up and cupped her chin. "The name is Haydon. 'My laird' is for everywhere except when we're alone."

Alone.

She shivered.

Why did that word terrify her? She cleared her throat again. "I wish to thank ye for chasing those men—and women—from the room."

He continued to run his finger up and down her cheek. "I could see it was making ye uncomfortable. I ne'er saw the need for it anyway. Maybe for the king and such, but I'll have no mon looking at my wife's uncovered body."

Tears sprang to her eyes. The switch with her sister, the fear of Haydon raising a fuss at the ceremony, the thought of sharing his bed, and now kindness from the mon she considered a brute was too much. "Thank ye."

One lone tear slid down her cheek.

Haydon wiped it with his thumb and left the bed to walk across the room to retrieve an ewer of wine and two goblets that had been left there. The sight of his naked, muscular backside as he moved fascinated her. Her hands itched to run her fingers over it, to feel the warmth and strength there. Not brave enough just yet, however, she closed her eyes as he turned and came back to the bed.

"Ye can open yer eyes now, Ainslee." He poured wine into the two cups and handed her one. "This will help to calm ye."

She nodded and took a sip.

Once more, he settled alongside her, watching her over the rim of his cup. "How old were ye when yer mam died?"

She drew circles on the bed coverings with her finger. "Not long after I was born." She looked up. "Da married again, but my stepmother died giving birth to my wee brother, who died shortly after that. Elsbeth and I were about eight or nine summers then, I believe."

"And he never married again after that?"

"Nay. He has a nephew who will inherit when Da passes away. Damian is a nice mon. He will do well."

He studied her carefully. "So, ye had no one speak to ye about what will happen tonight?"

"Nay." Another, larger sip of wine.

Haydon downed his wine in one gulp and set the cup aside on the small table next to the bed. "Drink up, lass, 'tis time ye learned what ye did when ye switched places with yer sister."

5

*H*aydon took the now empty goblet from Ainslee's hand.

Her shaking hand.

He'd had enough experience with women, but never had he bedded a virgin. Would she laugh if he told her he was nervous too? Bedding his wife was different than taking a tumble with one of the wenches in the castle. This initial introduction into intimate relations between husband and wife could set the tone for the rest of their marriage. He wanted her to find pleasure in the act, not simply endure it because it was her duty.

She looked so verra small in his bed. Small and terrified. All the reassurance in the world was not going to calm his nervous bride, so he might as well get on with it.

Reaching out, his fingers clamped over her trembling chin, and slowly lowered his head until his lips touched hers. Warm, soft, moist. When she didn't shudder or pull away, he wrapped his arms around her and pulled her lush body to his. There was far more to the lass than appeared while clothed.

To his surprise, she responded, pressing her lips to his, even shifting closer. He placed both his hands on her face and tilted her head to give him more access to the sweet taste of wine and something belonging to Ainslee. A scent of lavender drifted to him from her body.

His fingers wove their way into her hair, the silky strands sliding along his skin. Gently, he eased their bodies down until they were lying side by side, facing each other. He drew back, grazing his thumbs over her cheeks, his eyes shifting to the hammering pulse in her neck. Her eyes fluttered open, and she licked her lips, offering him a soft smile.

He was lost.

'Twas not the way it should be. His wife was an innocent, yet he saw in her eyes the same desire he felt. He traced her beautifully arched eyebrows with his finger. She closed her eyes and sighed. Aye, he'd married the right sister.

Slowly, he pulled at the bed covering that had slipped from her face to her shoulders. He sucked in a deep breath as the shapely beauty of her naked body taunted him. She moved to retrieve the coverlet, but he placed his hands over hers. "Nay, let me look at ye, lass."

He groaned as he gazed upon the most perfect breasts he'd ever seen. Plump, soft, white, with dark pink nipples, pouting, begging for his mouth.

He complied with their request, and Ainslee let out a soft moan as he nipped, licked, and suckled at her warm flesh. She was restless, had begun to shift her legs, her breathing increasing. "Aye, that feels good."

She gripped his head, pulling at his hair, arching her back, silently asking for more. He switched to her other breast as his hand wandered down her curves, gripping her arse, pulling her against his throbbing shaft.

He sensed a slight stiffness, so he moved his hand back up, caressing, soothing, stroking circles on her lower back, then once again moving to cover her magnificent bottom.

She was everything a mon could want in a bed partner. Lush, warm, beautiful, and responsive. Kissing his way up her warm, soft body to the tender skin under her ear, he grinned as she tugged on his hair and murmured "Nay. Doona stop."

"There's more to come, lass," he whispered. He nibbled, whispering her name, sucking on her ear lobe, teasing it with his teeth, then soothing it with his tongue.

No' one to wander from bed to bed, 'twas some time since he'd lain with a woman, and that, combined with the intense attraction he felt for the lass, was testing his control. Speeding things up would only cause problems for his wife, and if they were to have an active bed sport life, he needed to slowly introduce her to the joys and pleasures and not frighten or shock her.

'Twas a gracious thought to consider her innocence until her hand traveled from where she gripped his shoulder and wandered down his chest, pulling slightly on the hairs, twirling circles with her finger. "Yer hairs on yer chest are so different from the ones on yer head. Coarser." She gave a slight tug.

He pulled her in for another kiss, plastering her against him, teasing her lips with his tongue until she smiled and opened. He plunged in, once again finding all the sensitive parts of her mouth.

And her hand continued to wander down. He moaned, whether in pain or pleasure, he wasn't sure as she headed right to his shaft, gripping him with her warm, small hand. He sucked in a deep breath. "Ach, lass. That feels so good, but if ye continue, 'twill be over before it starts."

Leave it to his spirited wife to grin at his comments. And he was concerned that he would frighten her?

* * *

AINSLEE GRASPED the verra odd looking part of her husband's body. Hard and soft at the same time. Everything about his body was different from hers. Where he was straight, she was curvy. Where she was soft, he was hard, muscular. She felt safe in his arms, knowing he would never let anything happen to her.

She enjoyed more than anything how he hissed when she moved her hand up and down his shaft, squeezing slightly.

"Does that hurt?"

"Nay. It feels good. Too good, wife."

She was warm, verra, verra warm. She kicked the bedcovers off that had tangled around her feet. The warm brush of his fingers over her skin brought gooseflesh as his hands explored the lines of her waist, hips, moving behind her to grasp her bottom, pulling her against him once more. "Lass, yer driving me mad. This isna' gonna last very long, I'm afraid." He nibbled the skin where her neck and shoulder joined.

"Is that good or bad?"

He offered a soft laugh. "It depends. But I'll take care of ye first."

Not sure what that meant, she clasped his face with her hands and dragged him into a kiss. The mon was quite the kisser.

His hands lightly traced a path over her skin, settling at the place between her thighs. She jerked, startled at the intimate touch.

"Relax, wife."

He explored the area with his strong fingers, the wetness that surprised her making it easy for him to circle and stroke with his thumb. Ainslee grew restless, all of her attention centered on his fingers and what they were doing to her.

She put her arms around his neck, tugging lightly on the silk strands of his hair. Someone moaned, and she feared it was her.

"Do ye like that, lass?" Softly his breath fanned her face.

She nodded furiously, her head thrashing back and forth. "Aye. Doona stop this time."

"Ye are so wet for me." His eyes darkened dangerously as he studied her.

Assuming that was a good thing, given his tone, she was pleased that she wasn't doing this all wrong.

He put one of his large fingers inside her, but she was too taken with the feelings building in her to concern herself with that.

"Ach, lass, 'tis tight ye are. I must do more to prepare you." He scattered kisses along her jaw, over her face, under her ear. Her leg muscles kept tightening, and she pressed her center to his hand. "Please."

A second finger slipped in, but he continued to move his thumb over a bit of flesh she'd never noticed before. She felt something not too far off.

"Haydon, please I need something."

"I ken, lass." He lowered his head and suckled again on her breasts. First one, then the other. She held her breath as all the muscles in her body tightened, her attention directed on the area between her legs. She was reaching for something. "Haydon, please…"

"Aye, lass. Relax. 'Twill come if ye let me do the work."

No sooner had the words left his mouth than a strong wave of pleasure like she'd never felt before, nor knew was even possible, washed over her. She bucked against his hand, drawing out the amazing feeling.

Once she regained her senses, she lay panting, her chest heaving. The air had left her body and all her bones had truly melted. She felt as though she might never walk again. Just as she was settling in for a nice relaxing sleep, Haydon rolled over and within seconds, his hard body was on top of hers.

"'Tis not over?" Was that her voice? She shook her head; she sounded so sluggish.

"Nay, lass," he laughed. "'Tis my turn now."

He shifted, settling snugly into the space between her legs. She felt her breasts crush against his muscular chest. Once more, he took her mouth in a burning kiss, stirring in her something she'd thought she'd finished with. Her body squirmed beneath his, and she pressed her hips against his, a low moan coming from somewhere deep inside.

With a groan, he placed his hands underneath her

bottom and shifted her up. "This might hurt for a bit, lass, but 'twill be over soon."

"Hurt?" Before she could grasp what he'd said, he shoved forward, and she squeaked as a sharp pain brought tears to her eyes. She tried to wiggle backward. "Stop. 'Tis hurting."

He stopped, and with a half-smile, stared into her eyes. "Be at ease, *mo chridhe*. Give it a moment just relax."

Realizing he had shoved his shaft into the opening at the place between her legs, she was reminded of the time she'd seen horses mating. At least Haydon hadn't turned her over and pushed at her from behind.

The pain receded, and as he continued to slowly slide in and out, she relaxed and found the stroking quite nice. In fact, more than quite nice since the feeling from before was building again. "Haydon," she gasped. "'Tis good."

"Aye, lass, 'tis most certainly good." His mouth covered hers hungrily as he held her head, moving it to take the kiss deeper. Within minutes, his body movements became frantic, and he pulled her close, burying his head between her head and shoulder, mumbling her name and other endearments.

She felt a warm rush inside her, then he slowed and stopped. After a few minutes, she felt his lips brush her brow as he shifted his body and pulled her snug to his side. They both lay panting, Haydon lightly running his fingers up and down her back.

As their breathing returned to normal, Ainslee looked over at Haydon who was studying her. "What are ye thinking?"

He reached out and smoothed her hair away from her forehead. "Ye pleased me, wife."

Annoyance rose in her chest. The arrogant oaf. She boldly met his eyes. "That's it? That's all ye have to say? I pleased ye? Well, mayhaps ye did not please me."

Her words seemed to amuse him. "Is that so, lass? Yer sighs and moaning told me otherwise."

A flush began in her middle and rose to her face. Had he not already said he was pleased, she would think he had imagined he'd not married a pure woman. However, she'd found it hard not to respond to his touch.

When she shivered, Haydon leaned forward and drew the bedcovers up over them. Once again, he pulled her to his side, tucking her securely against him. She rested her head on his warm chest and sighed. All she wanted now was a good night's sleep. Tomorrow, she would deal with this new life she'd thrust herself into.

Mayhaps things would not be so bad, after all.

6

*H*aydon spent the first few minutes of the new day staring at his sleeping wife. His unintended wife.

Now that the frenzy of the wedding had passed, he had time to think on his new life. He smiled as he remembered looking at Ainslee the minute she entered the Kirk. He knew immediately something was off. Then when she looked him in the eye, which was something he knew Elsbeth would never do, his suspicions were confirmed.

The lasses had switched places.

Last night's activities right here in the bed proved him right in no' stopping the ceremony. The shy, nervous Elsbeth would never have given him the pleasure and satisfaction he'd received from Ainslee.

He shook his head and laughed as he threw the coverlet off and strode to the large wooden chest on the other side of the room. He washed, then dressed, and with Ainslee still in deep slumber, left the room to break his fast.

With the wedding nonsense over, he needed to set up a meeting for the clans. There were many in the area angry at the defeat of Charles II at Worcester and what they considered the invasion of the Commonwealth with its rules and taxes. Further resentment was the occupation of the English army in the Lowlands and the attempt to incorporate the Highlands under British rule.

Earlier in the year, William Cunningham, 8th Earl of Glencairn, had proposed a rebellion against the Commonwealth. A hatred for the British resided in nearly every Highlander's heart, so it hadn't been hard to rally the clans to join Glencairn.

Now it was Haydon's job to begin preparations by uniting the clans in the area and obtain promises of supplies, swords, and horses for the rebellion. Since he dinna think his wedding was the proper place to bring up the rebellion, he would need to contact them as soon as possible.

Conall was already at the table in the great hall where most meals were eaten. When his da and mam had been alive, the family would eat the last meal of the day in a separate room, but once Mam passed, Haydon had done away with the tradition.

Conall slapped him on the back as he settled alongside him. "How's the bridegroom this morning?" He leaned in and winked. "Did the lass wear ye out, then? Or, since she's missing, mayhaps you wore her out?"

"Do no' speak of my wife," he groused.

"That bad, aye?"

Haydon stared at his brother. "I will say this once, and ye will cease to e're mention it again. I am verra pleased with my wife and doona expect you to question our private life again. Do ye understand?"

Conall held up his hands in surrender but seemed to have a problem holding in his laughter. "Aye, my laird."

The mon could be most annoying, but no better brother could a laird ask for. They'd fought side-by-side and back-to-back many times, and he expected to do so in the future. Especially with talk of a rebellion.

"Can I ask ye one thing that has naught to do with yer private life?"

Haydon nodded at the young lass who poured his cup of ale and placed a trencher in front of him. "Aye."

"How did ye end up married to Ainslee when the betrothal was for ye and the other lass?"

"'Tis nay concern of yers. Just ken what's done is done, and ye doona need to question it."

"Elsbeth is a fine lass."

Haydon's raised eyebrows at his brother was his only answer.

"Laird, will we be working the list today?" Malcolm Sutherland, Haydon's cousin and second right-hand mon approached them.

"And why would we no' be practicing?"

"Well, since yer wedding was yesterday…"

"And?"

Conall burst out laughing. "If yer about to ask the laird if he is able to swing a sword today, due to last night's activities, I would turn right around and leave. Quickly."

Haydon glowered at his brother. Then, turning to Malcolm, said, "Start the training. I have messages to send to the other clans. I'll join ye when I'm finished."

Conall and Malcolm both left the hall as Haydon downed his meal and then made his way to the solar, the best room to use for writing, with the window facing the morning sun.

He drew out a piece of parchment and began the task of convincing the clan lairds to join him in preparing for the rebellion. Once finished, he called for a messenger to dispatch the missives, then joined his men in the list.

* * *

AINSLEE SLOWLY OPENED HER EYES, for a moment confused as to where she was. Then a smile broke out on her face when she remembered. The wedding switch, the raucous celebration that followed, and then the most surprising and best time of the day when she and Haydon had become husband and wife, truly.

Since his side of the bed was empty and cold, he must have risen early and allowed her to take an extra sleep.

Anxious to start her day as the mistress of the keep, she swung her legs over the side of the bed and stood. Although a bit sore from the previous night's activities, it didn't take long for her to wash, dress, and head to the great hall.

She felt a twinge of disappointment when Haydon was not sitting at the table, breaking his fast. Then she shook her head at her silly thoughts. Theirs was no great love match, she had merely substituted herself for another bride he didn't love either. And the last thing she wanted from this marriage was love. She would not put herself under the mon's control.

She wandered into the kitchen in search of food and to see if she could find out where Elsbeth was. She hadn't seen her since the women dragged her upstairs to prepare her for the bedding the night before. It would have been nice to have her sister's comforting presence while she awaited Haydon.

"Good morning, my lady." A rather stout woman stood in front of the fireplace, stirring something that didn't really smell all that good. That was a reminder she needed to do a bit of changing the fare at the keep.

"Good morning to you. May I ask yer name?"

The woman did a slight curtsy. "The name is Margie, my lady. Margie Sutherland."

"It is a pleasure to meet you, Margie." She looked around the kitchen at three other kitchen maids at various tables, busy chopping vegetables and plucking feathers from some fowl.

She could see dirt under the fingernails of the one plucking the feathers, and the table with the vegetables on it was dirty, looking as though it hadn't had a good scrub since the building had been erected.

It appeared she had a lot of work to do. She turned to Margie. "Are there mayhaps some oatcakes or such I can have to break my fast?"

'Twas surprising that it was not offered when she entered the kitchen. It seemed there was more work to be done than cleaning the place up and inspecting the larders.

"Aye, my lady. I have some oatcakes left from the morning meal. Ye can find them over there," Margie gestured with her head in the direction of a table pushed up against the wall. Also, quite dirty, with what looked like blood smeared on it. Her stomach turned, and she decided she wasn't hungry after all.

"Is it possible to have some tea?"

"Now?" Margie said.

Ainslee was growing angry. This was no way to treat the lady of the manor. When she and Elsbeth ran their father's keep no one, especially someone of status—like the laird's wife—would be treated in such a way.

Deciding she would need more information before she began her assault on the kitchen, she waved the woman off. "Nay. I'll just have a bit of ale."

Margie nodded and returned to her task. Ainslee poured ale from a large pitcher and took a small sip before she committed to drinking the entire cup. Whoever made the clan's ale was much more skilled than the women doing the cooking.

After quenching her thirst, she approached Margie again. "Where is yer herb garden?"

"Doona have one." She never lifted her head but continued to stir the pot.

Ainslee was appalled. "No herb garden?"

"Nay. Dried up some time ago. After Lady Sutherland passed, Lady Donella took over managing the keep. She dinna have an interest in the kitchen." She shrugged. "Or anything else either."

Conversation here in the kitchen was only frustrating her, so she decided the best thing to occupy her time was to find her sister and talk over what she'd found so far. They'd shared the running of Da's keep and always did their tasks together. Mayhaps Elsbeth might have some ideas on how to straighten things out.

Rather than bother the cook again and receive another sharp retort that would merely annoy her, she decided to take a stroll around the keep to see what she'd missed when they'd arrived for the wedding. At the time, she and Elsbeth were so nervous about their switch, they hadn't paid much attention to anything except the overwhelming presence of Laird Sutherland.

A rather warm glow started in her middle when she thought of her husband and the night before. Mayhaps he was correct, and he wasn't such a brute. Mayhaps she'd made the best decision of her life when she and Elsbeth switched places.

The crofters and tinkers were set up outside the keep in the inner bailey. So, starting there to find Elsbeth would be a good idea since her sister loved visiting the crofters and merchants.

With her stomach grumbling from emptiness, she stopped at a stand where a woman was selling wonderful smelling oatcakes dripping with honey. She closed her eyes with a sigh as she bit into the delightful treat. It was doubtful similar tasting cakes would be offered by Margie.

As she licked her fingers, she continued to go from cart to cart until she finally spotted Elsbeth. Once again, she thanked her da for allowing Elsbeth to stay with her. Since he was so interested in getting her married, mayhaps one of the men here would take an interest in her.

"Elsbeth!" She called her name as her sister headed toward the keep.

Elsbeth turned and broke into a huge smile. They hurried toward each other and hugged. Ainslee leaned back. "Where have you been? I haven't seen you since that crowd of ladies dragged me from the wedding festivities."

They linked arms and began to walk. "I saw them take

ye, but I was dancing at the time and thought I would join them when the music stopped. However, by the time it stopped, the group was gone, and I had no idea where the laird's bedchamber was." She grinned at her. "I didn't think 'twould be wise for me to ask."

Ainslee laughed. "Ye are probably right."

Elsbeth's cheeks grew red. "Um, how did it go? I mean, are ye well?"

Ainslee thought briefly of their time together in Haydon's large, comfortable bed and smiled. "Aye, I am well."

They looked at each other and giggled.

Elsbeth's face grew serious. "Ye must speak with Da. I ken ye told me last eve that he said I could stay here for a bit. This morn, he claimed he never said so."

"Aye, he did say so, but he was well into his cups at the time. I'll remind him of his promise. Do ye ken where he is?"

"I think after taking a bit more ale this morn, he said he was going to watch the men training at the lists."

Ainslee had been trying to think of a reason to take a stroll to the lists. She would love to see Haydon swinging his sword again with all that glistening golden skin and those powerful muscles. She thought back to the time at Lochwood Tower when she watched him from her window, and then grew annoyed when he caught her. And had the nerve to smile and bow.

The arrogant oaf.

"There is something we need to discuss once we remind Da of his promise."

Elsbeth turned to her. "What is that? You look most serious."

"Aye. The keep is not being run properly. Mam would have a lot to say about how things are here. Do ye ken I went to the kitchen to get something to break my fast, and the cook acted as though I had no right to require food? And when I asked for tea, she questioned me as to why it had to be then, like she was far too busy to fix tea for the laird's wife."

"Ach. No' good, I'm afraid."

Ainslee shook her head. "Nay. I also noticed the rushes could use a change in a few rooms."

They continued past a table with numerous ribbons on it. They both stopped and viewed the offerings. "Now that ye mention it, the bedchamber we shared before the wedding has enough dust to build a wall." Elsbeth glanced over at her sister. "Who's been in charge?"

Ainslee held up a lovely green ribbon. "Haydon said while his mam was sick and then after she died, his sister, Donella, was supposed to take over. I doona think she's up to the task, though."

"Is she the lass with the long, dark braid who seemed bored by the entire wedding yesterday?"

Ainslee reached into her pouch and withdrew a coin, handing it to the crofter. "Aye. Long, dark hair, pretty face, seems to be a bit absent in her head." She looked quickly at the crofter and then at Elsbeth. "Doona repeat what I said."

"Nay."

The sound of swords clashing caught their attention as they drew closer to the lists. Ainslee felt her heart speed up at the thought of seeing her husband again. She really needed to stop this fascination she had with the mon. Aye, he was easy to look at, and 'twas hard not to admire all the braw the mon possessed, but she needed to keep reminding herself that the worst thing she could do was fall in love with the arrogant oaf. The control he would have o'er her would make her miserable.

They turned the corner of the keep to the sight of dozens of men swinging swords. Sun shone off their backs, glistening with sweat. Her eyes went immediately to the largest mon in the field.

Haydon battled a warrior she didn't ken, who must have said something to him, because her husband turned and looked in her direction just as his partner brought his sword up under Haydon's.

The laird's sword flew into the air.

7

Hearing Ainslee's name from Barclay had distracted Haydon. 'Twas not a good thing to happen to a warrior, even if he was training. He swiped his sword up from the ground, motioned for Barclay to train with another mon, and stormed over to where his wife and her sister stood.

He almost laughed at the difference between the two. Elsbeth's eyes grew wide as he got closer to them, and her face paled. She whispered something to Ainslee and scurried away. His wife, on the other hand, stood there, peaceful as ye please even though he knew the glower on his face had intimidated men twice her size.

"What are ye doing here? Doona you ken we're training? Dinna ye get enough of watching me from yer window at the Johnstone keep?"

She crossed her arms under her breasts. He refused to allow himself *that* distraction. "Pfft! Think ye I came to admire yer scrawny body? Nay. I came to find my da who I was told is here."

Haydon leaned in closer, not sure if he should be amused or angered at her reference to his 'scrawny body'. "Women are no' allowed on the lists."

The lass had the nerve to lean in too. "I'm no' on the lists. I'm merely looking for my da."

"I have no intention of arguing with ye, wife." He pointed away from the list. " I am yer laird, and I order ye to leave. Ye are to go now and see yer da later."

It appeared Ainslee gave a thought to defying him, but in the end, she turned and strode off, her skirts flying in the air as she made her way.

Haydon shook his head and wondered if he should admire the lass for her courage in facing him or give her another tongue lashing for arguing with him. Mayhaps a thorough reminder of her place as his wife, given in their bedchamber later, might finish with the lass unleashing all that passion in another, more pleasurable way.

He grinned at the thought and returned to the lists, ready to take down Barclay, else the mon become too confident.

AFTER HOURS OF PRACTICE, Haydon had no sooner entered the keep than Donella approached him.

"Good afternoon, sister. I take it all is well?"

"Aye," she smiled. "Ainslee and her sister have taken over the running of the keep. 'Tis grateful I am to ye for finding a wife, and grateful to Ainslee for bringing her sister with her."

Apparently, there weren't too many who knew of the lasses' deception when it came to the wedding. 'Twas just as well. The lass was now his wife, and he would tolerate no lack of respect for the laird's wife.

"Have the lasses been busy then?" He hoped they would begin with the kitchen. The food could certainly be improved. When his mam had been alive, the food had been plentiful and tasty. Margie had not been the cook then, but old Mrs. McFee had passed away not long after Mam, and Donella had found Margie.

"Aye. I think Ainslee spent some time in the kitchens, and the last I saw Elsbeth, she was speaking with the chamber maids."

Haydon was happy to have relieved his wee sister from the burden of running the castle at her young age. He knew at fifteen summers, she should be more than ready to take on the responsibilities of marriage and running a mon's home, but to him, she was still a child. Despite her age and Mam's attempt to train her, Donella had always been a dreamer.

"Well, sister, I am glad ye are no longer burdened with the duties."

The lass skipped off like no more than a bairn. He shook his head, wondering if he was doing her a favor, or if he should insist she follow Ainslee around and learn what she needed to know to one day marry.

He took the stone stairs two at a time to the second floor where the bedchambers were.

The castle had been home to the Sutherlands for more than five hundred years. Parts of it were constructed during various centuries, leaving the keep and surrounding buildings a patchwork of designs. But to Haydon, it had always been home, somewhere to protect and to one day raise a family.

Hopefully, with now having a wife, he would be able to secure the lands with an heir.

He came to an abrupt halt when he entered the laird's bedchamber. All the furniture had been pushed to one side of the room. Several servants, directed by his wife were sweeping up rushes, cleaning walls and tearing down bed hangings.

In the middle of the mess stood his wife, waving her arms and shouting orders.

"What the devil is going on here?" He'd come to his bedchamber for a wash and change of clothes before descending to the great hall for the evening meal. Instead, he found chaos.

"This room is a disgrace, my laird," Ainslee said. "'Tis in need of a thorough cleaning."

"Now? When it grows close to suppertime? This will no' be ready for sleeping this eve."

"Nay. I arranged for us to sleep in the smaller chamber." She gestured with her head to the door that connected the main bedchamber with a smaller one. The main one had always been the laird's, and the smaller one had belonged to the lady of the manor.

Since throughout the years many lairds had lemans, they would use their bedchamber for those visits, and would do their duty with their wife in the smaller chamber to procure an heir. Since Haydon had no intention of securing the services of a leman, he'd decided before he'd even married that he and his wife would sleep and do whatever else they enjoyed in the laird's large, comfortable bed.

Still burning from their encounter in the lists, he pointed to the door. "Everyone out."

Apparently, his voice was enough to rattle the servants but not his wife, who stood glaring at him, her arms crossed. Her favorite pose.

"We were making progress. I doona understand why ye would chase them all out."

He waved his finger at her. "Doona keep questioning me, wife. I am yer husband and yer laird, and what I say is the final word on the matter. Do ye understand?" He began to strip off his sweaty clothes. "If ye want to be a good wife, have someone fetch a bowl of warm water. I want to wash before I dress."

She tapped her foot, seeming to naysay him, but eventually, she turned and stomped from the room.

He laughed as the door slammed shut. Yes, life with Lady Ainslee Sutherland will be quite the ride.

* * *

ARROGANT OAF.

Ainslee made her way downstairs. With the servants busy setting up for supper, she decided to fetch the water and cloths herself. Besides, she wished to speak with Haydon about the mess the keep was in.

Every room she and Elsbeth had visited was discouraging. Dirty, smelly rushes. Furniture, walls, and draperies that hadn't been cleaned in ages. Bed linens in dire need of washing.

Apparently, Lady Sutherland had been quite sick for some time before she passed away, so Donella had been in charge—such as it was—for a longer time than the lass was capable of.

It annoyed her, also, because her main mission had

been to address the food. But no one could be comfortable in a home that was dirty and filthy. They'd seen rodent droppings, dead insects, and other undefinable things in just about every room.

She'd learned from Lochwood Tower's chatelaine that many illnesses could be prevented by keeping things clean. Aggie Johnstone had been an excellent chatelaine before Ainslee and Elsbeth had taken over when Aggie grew too old.

She managed to get the hot water without disturbing Margie very much and also located two clean cloths. As she hurried from the room, she took a sniff of the meat sitting on a table, ready to be cut into portions. Another uneventful supper. But then, if they had no herb garden, it was no wonder the food was tasteless at best.

Haydon had stripped down to his leather trews. And nothing else. Ainslee carried the water over to the table next to the fireplace and attempted to ignore her husband's strong chest, with the dusting of dark, curly hair. Hair she'd run her fingers through the night before.

"Seen enough, lass?" He had the nerve to grin at her. She hated how he kept catching her staring at him. Most likely he'd had women staring at him his whole life.

"No' much to see."

He burst into laughter and dipped one of the cloths into the water. He rubbed soap onto the cloth and handed it to her.

"What is it?"

"Isna' a wife's job to wash her husband's back?"

With a smirk, she took the cloth from his hand. "Sit."

Her breath caught as she ran her palm over his warm, muscular back. There were several scars from battles fought, but instead of detracting from the mon's appeal, they only added to it.

She rinsed the soap off with the other cloth, taking her time, smoothing the cloth over his skin.

"Ah, lass, that feels good." He reached over his shoulder and pulled her onto his lap. She fell with a thump, her arms automatically going around his neck. "I'm no' finished."

Instead of answering, he dipped his head and took her lips in a soft, warm, moist kiss. All thoughts of protest left her head when he continued his assault on her mouth.

Just as she settled into the kiss, there was a loud thumping on the door. Ainslee jumped off his lap, knocking the bowl of water onto the floor. Haydon growled and stomped over to the door, flinging it open.

Evan Sutherland, a young mon recently moved up to full warrior in the past few weeks stood at the door, looking anxiously over Haydon's shoulder at Ainslee cleaning up the mess the water had made.

"Ah, 'tis sorry I am to disturb ye, Laird, but a messenger has arrived from Glencairn and wishes to return with an answer."

Haydon took a clean leine from the hook near the door, shrugged into it, and fastened it as he left the room without a backward glance at Ainslee.

She sighed, used to a mon's abrupt departure. Da would oftentimes do the same to the women in the family. Sometimes it seemed as though politics ruled their lives.

She'd heard rumblings of an uprising against the Commonwealth. It seemed her entire life there were talks of rebellion. Da had fought in several skirmishes. She wished London would just leave them alone. Highlanders were verra good at taking care of themselves.

Too many times, she imagined the world would be a better place—aye, a more peaceful place to be sure—if women were in charge instead of men, always blustering with self-importance.

With a sigh, she gathered up the water bowl and cloths and returned to the great hall. Haydon was nowhere to be seen, so she returned the items to the kitchen just in time to see Margie slap one of the young servants in the face. The blow was so powerful the lass fell to her knees.

"See here," Ainslee said as she rushed forward. "There will be no slapping in the kitchen." She walked over to the servant and helped her up. "Be on yer way, lass."

She turned to Margie who was glowering at her. "'Tis my kitchen, my lady, and I decide how the servants are treated."

"Nay, Margie. 'Tis yer laird's kitchen, and as his wife, I decide how the servants are to be dealt with." She waved her finger in the woman's face. "And I state again. There will be no slapping."

All had grown silent with the altercation. Margie turned back to the pot she was stirring. "Get back to work, all of ye." She waved her spirtle at Ainslee. "'Tis with the laird I shall be speaking tomorrow."

Ainslee was stunned, sure Haydon would take Margie to task. 'Twas no way to treat the laird's wife.

Once she arrived at the great hall, she saw Elsbeth sitting at the family table, along with Conall and Haydon. Donella was nowhere in sight.

"Was the messenger good or bad news?" Ainslee asked as she settled alongside her husband and took a sip of ale.

Haydon looked at her with raised brows. "'Tis no concern of yers, wife."

Elsbeth nudged her in her side. She looked at her sister who shook her head slightly. "Ye forget yer place, sister. Ye should know from Da that you doona question the laird."

"The laird is my husband."

"Aye. That he is." Elsbeth looked over Ainslee's shoulder at the mon. "But it appears he doona wishes to discuss this with ye. Later, mayhaps. But I think based on what happened earlier at the lists that he'd like to keep his wife and the rest of his life separate."

Ainslee's temper flared. "And now *ye* wish to tell me how to be a wife? Are ye so skilled at the task, then?"

She immediately regretted her words at the look on Elsbeth's face. The mon was driving her mad, and she was taking it out on her beloved sister.

Ainslee looked over at her husband, huddled with Conall and her da, of all people. Even though Da was not part of the Sutherland clan, he got to listen to what Haydon was saying.

The life of a woman was frustrating at times. Then the thought came to her that mayhaps Elsbeth would have been the best wife for Haydon after all.

She took another gulp of her ale, thinking of the bed sport the night before. She grinned. "Nay."

8

Haydon stood, stretched, then shook himself out before leaving his solar in search of Ainslee. He'd spent the prior three hours hunched over his desk, going over messages that had been returned o'er the last several days from those he'd sent out, and then discussing and strategizing with his brother and top aides about their part in a possible uprising.

He was still not convinced it was a good idea for his clan to be involved in Glencairn's plans. The main issues with the Commonwealth rules affected the Lowlands, like his wife's clan, the Johnstone's. The Highlanders, while not immune, did not have to put up with British soldiers everywhere like the border clans did.

At present, he was going along with the idea, but he needed time to clear his head and consider the consequences his clan would suffer should the uprising fail. The British had proven ruthless with their enemies.

With his head in a muddle, he'd decided to seek out Ainslee, and maybe the two of them could go for a ride.

TO DECEIVE A HIGHLANDER

He needed to show her more of the lands and the village attached to it.

His search led him to the bedchambers and the great hall. Servants were busy—busier than he'd seen them in a long while—but no one knew where Ainslee was.

The kitchen hadn't turned up his wife either. "I doona ken where yer wife is." Margie turned her back on him and continued to stir a large cauldron over the fire.

Stunned at the cook's attitude, he said, "Doona turn yer back on me, woman."

She placed the spirtle on the table next to the fireplace and turned to him. She rested her hands on her considerable middle. "I apologize, my laird. I am verra busy and canno' help ye find yer wife."

He glared at her. "I dinna ask ye to find the lass, I only asked if you kenned where she was. She was to do some work in the kitchens today."

Margie shrugged. "Aye, she was here for a bit, but left a while ago. Dinna say where she was going. And I dinna ask."

More interested in finding Ainslee than in upbraiding the surly cook, he left the kitchen with a note in his head to deal with her soon. 'Twould never do to have a servant speak to him in that manner. He'd also like to know where it was Donella had found the woman when their prior cook had died. It appeared not only was the cook unskilled in food preparation but had no idea how to conduct herself when speaking with her laird.

Finally, frustrated with his lack of success, he left the keep. He would take a ride by himself. 'Twould have been better to have his wife's company. Especially since their marriage, they'd only seen each other for supper and then bed. Not that he minded the bedding part, but he needed to speak with her to at least find out what she was doing with the keep.

It seemed every room he'd gone into in search of her was in disarray. Window coverings and wall tapestries down, breezes blowing through the uncovered windows in all the bedchambers, turning the rooms frigidly cold. Old, smelly rushes had been swept out of each room and piled in the corridor to be brought outside and burned.

Pushing all of that aside, he headed to the stable. The air was cool with a light wind. Spring in the Highlands was unpredictable. Warm and sunny one moment, then dark clouds would roll in, the temperature drop, and even icy rain could fall.

He entered the dark stable to see Broderick, the old stablemaster, rubbing oil on a bridle. "Do ye want yer horse, Laird?"

"Aye. Off for a short ride."

He laid the bridle aside and walked the length of the stable to where Haydon's horse, Demon was kept. "Not too long ago, yer wife took one of the horses and left." Broderick spoke over his shoulder as he led the horse out to be tacked.

"Who was with her?"

Broderick shrugged. "No one. She requested a horse, then high-tailed it out of here as soon as it was ready. Didn't say where she was headed."

A tightness started in his stomach and soon consumed him. The woman was daft if she thought she could ride around without an escort. These were dangerous times, and he had no intention of finding his wife's battered body dumped in the woods somewhere.

"What direction was she headed?" he asked as he swung his leg over Demon.

"The village."

Haydon nodded and turned Demon in that direction. He kept an eye out the entire ride to the village but did not come across Ainslee. Or her dead, assaulted body. However, his anger grew as time passed and he didn't see her heading back to the keep.

By the time he reached the village he was in a turmoil of anger and fear. Never before had he felt such fear for someone's welfare. 'Twas an unsettling feeling and one he wasn't happy with. A wife should ken her place and stay there, no' wander about and cause her husband annoyance.

He headed for the tavern, hoping the lass had stopped there for a bite to eat.

The room was smoky, dark, and despite the fire, cold. Once his eyes adjusted, he searched the room. Sitting at a table in a shadowed corner sat his wife, looking as happy as a bairn, sipping an ale.

Ach! The lass would be the death of him.

She looked up as he approached her table. He pulled out a chair and slumped into it, staring at her. "What the devil are ye doing, Ainslee?"

Glancing into her cup, she said, "Having a bit of ale?"

"Doona make a joke of this." He waved his finger at her, resisting his urge to throttle her. "Ye are not allowed to leave the keep without my permission."

She straightened in her chair and glared at him. "I doona believe what I just heard, so I will repeat it for my tired mind. *I cannot leave the keep without yer permission?*"

"Aye." He glanced away and signaled the serving wench.

Ainslee continued to stare at him, her mouth open. Haydon reached over and put his finger under her chin. "Close yer mouth, lass."

She leaned over, her finger tapping the table. "I am a prisoner then?"

He waved her off. "Of course no'. Ye just cannot go wandering around without an escort. Since I provide the escorts, ye need my permission before ye leave."

Considering how easy he'd let her off and congratulating himself on a job well done in wife handling, he took a large gulp of ale.

Apparently, his wife didn't agree.

"Haydon, I did no' require my da's permission to leave the keep."

He shook his head. "A poor choice on his part, to be sure. But, 'tis no matter. Do no' argue. I am yer laird. 'Tis my order." He gulped more ale.

* * *

AINSLEE'S FINGERS itched to toss the rest of her ale into her arrogant husband's face. Not leave the keep without his permission! She had to admit that perhaps going off by herself had not been the wisest of ideas since a woman unescorted could run into all sorts of difficult situations.

However, she'd been so verra angry at her exchange with Margie in the kitchen, that all she could think about was getting away before she disgraced herself and let out a string of foul words unfit for the laird's wife to speak.

When she lived at Lochwood Tower, she would merely

ask one of the stablemen to accompany her on rides without seeking permission from anyone. No one had been around the stable except for old Broderick, and she had no intention of asking the mon to put aside his work to accompany her.

And from what she'd seen since her marriage, her husband was much too busy to be troubled by any requests from her to accompany her on a ride.

"Now that's settled, I wish to speak with ye about the goings-on in the keep." Again, her husband glared at her. She huffed. Dinna the mon ever grow weary of lecturing her?

And just like a mon to think giving an order settled things. Ainslee nodded, not wishing to continue that discussion lest she did dump her ale over the mon's head. "Aye?"

"I appreciate ye taking an interest in the place, and I ken wee Donella wasn't up to the task, but it seems to me all the rooms are being cleaned at the same time."

"Aye. All the bedchambers. They were filthy, Haydon. The rushes hadn't been changed in ages and were full of bugs and animal droppings. 'Tis not a healthy place. 'Tis a wonder ye haven't been plagued with sickness."

He pointed a finger at her. "I ken yer in charge of household matters, but I am the one to make the decisions."

"Ye make the decisions? Should I run about the keep searching for ye every time I want to remove a room full of filthy rushes?"

His eyes narrowed. "Ye are misunderstanding." Another sip of ale. "See that the bedchambers are finished first."

She gritted her teeth. "Is that an order, my laird?"

"Aye. An order."

Ainslee stood. "'Tis time for me to return to the keep." She moved to walk away from the table, but he reached out and grabbed her hand. "Nay. Ye'll no' be returning alone. Sit yerself down. I would have a meat pie before we leave."

"Do ye hear yerself, Haydon? Everything that comes out of yer mouth is an order."

"Aye." He downed the rest of his ale and waved at the serving lass. "A meat pie and another ale." He looked at Ainslee. "Do ye wish a meat pie?"

Ach, she would love to say no and sit there and sulk while he ate, but she truly did love the smell of the pies, and knowing what she faced back at the keep for supper, 'twas a much better idea to eat here.

"Aye."

He patted her hand. "See. That's better, lass."

She closed her eyes. The mon had no idea how he sounded. Or mayhaps he did and was so used to giving orders, he didn't see anything odd about speaking to his wife as if she were one of his warriors. Or a bairn.

They ate their food in silence. She considered relating the story of her conflict with Margie but decided she would gain more respect among the clan if she handled keep matters without engaging the help of the laird. At least that was her thoughts before he 'ordered' her to come to him with decisions.

"'Tis time to go, lass. It appears the pleasant day is turning sour." Haydon looked out the window across from their table at the growing clouds and wind that had picked up since she'd entered the tavern.

"Aye."

He dropped coins on the table, and placing his hand at her lower back, they left. When they reached their horses, he undid his plaid and draped it over her shoulders. "Ye'll need this, lass." He looked up at the sky again. "'Tis turning colder. We need to hurry."

Grateful for the extra warmth, since she still hadn't gotten used to the cooler temperatures in the Highlands compared to the Lowlands, she flinched when his large, warm hands wrapped around her waist, and he plopped her onto the horse's back.

She adjusted the plaid around her shoulders. Sometimes the mon could be most thoughtful. He was truly a puzzle, lecturing her one minute, then looking out for her comfort the next. "Thank ye."

He smiled at her in the way that made her insides grow warm. The arrogant oaf must have noticed her reaction because his warm smile turned to male satisfaction.

Not waiting for him to mount his horse, she kicked the sides of the animal and galloped off. Within seconds Haydon was alongside her.

It felt good, the wind in her hair, the chill on her face, the cold air stinging her eyes. She yelled over the rising wind, "I'll race ye."

Haydon's eyes grew wide, no doubt surprised that she would even consider taking on the laird in a horse race. No matter. She dinna intend to win, she only wanted to have the feel of the competition.

'Twas obvious from the start that Haydon was holding his horse back, since they remained neck and neck. About a mile from the stable, he yelled something that Ainslee dinna hear, and his horse took off as if shot from a cannon.

She tried her best, but Demon far surpassed her mount, and Haydon arrived at the stable well before her. He jumped from his horse, grinning when she arrived. He grabbed her around the waist again and plopped her in front of him. He smoothed back the hair that had fallen across her face during the race, the ribbon that had held it in place floating somewhere in the wind. "'Twas a good race, lass."

She rested her hands on his shoulders and looked up at him. "Aye. Would it have been so good had ye lost?"

"I ne'er lose." He slung his arm around her shoulders and pulled her close to him. The warmth from his body took away the chill she'd gotten from the ride. She also once again experienced the little flutters in her stomach.

He lowered his head, and his warm mouth covered hers. Within seconds the kiss went from something warm and comfortable to hot and passionate. Ainslee leaned into his body as he used his tongue to mimic the mating act.

Before she was ready, he pulled back and stared at her, his eyes dark with desire. "Aye, lass, 'twas a good race, but I'm ready for a different kind of sport."

They arrived at the keep just as the first drops of rain hit her on the nose. Ainslee entered the great hall to see Elsbeth standing in the middle of the room, wringing her hands.

Her sister took one look at Ainslee and Haydon and burst into tears.

9

Ainslee rushed to her sister's side. "Elsbeth, what is wrong?"

Haydon stood back as the lass wailed and hugged his wife without saying a word. He waited almost a full minute before joining the lasses. He took hold of Ainslee's shoulders and pulled her back.

She frowned at him, but before she could say anything, he turned to Elsbeth. "What has ye so distraught, lass?"

Elsbeth took a deep breath. "I had a bit of a problem with Margie, and I'm afraid I upset her."

Haydon drew in a breath. The cook who had given him a hard time earlier. The woman did not seem to be the type to get upset over anything the lass could say to her. Insult her, throw something at her, that seemed to be more of Margie's temperament. Elsbeth was meek and timid. Too much so for his liking.

"Ye need to calm down and tell me what happened."

Ainslee wrapped her arm around her sister's shoulder. "Tell him, Elsbeth."

The lass leaned into Ainslee's side and whispered in her ear. Haydon tried to be patient since the lass would only become more distressed if he bellowed at her, but he was truly becoming twitchier by the minute.

Ainslee shook her head and smoothed her sister's hair. "Nay. The laird willnae toss ye out."

Finally losing patience with the nonsense, Haydon said, "I'll be tossing ye both out if ye doona tell me why yer weeping all over my wife."

Elsbeth gulped and straightened but continued to stare at the floor. "I made a suggestion to Margie about the food preparation, and she became most irritated. She ordered me from the kitchen and said if I returned, she would quit."

"Tis all? No one is lying dead in the kitchen? The place hasn't burned down?"

"Nay."

Haydon shook his head and stomped away, mumbling to himself about the silliness of women. As he barged into the large room, several pairs of eyes looked up from their work.

Except Margie.

He stopped in front of the woman. "Ye are finished here. Leave now for yer home and do no' return."

The woman turned, her hands on her hips. "And who will do the cooking?"

"Certainly no' ye." He pointed to the back door of the room. "If ye aren't gone in twenty seconds, I'll toss ye out myself."

Margie whipped the apron off, dropped it to the floor, and tramped from the room, slamming the door behind her.

He looked around the room, all the kitchen maids staring at him. "Who can cook?"

They all looked at each other, but no one spoke.

He looked in the cauldron Margie had been stirring. "What is this?"

No one spoke.

He leaned in and sniffed. Not exactly horrible, but whatever the contents were certainly did not tempt him to taste it. "Who is in charge when Margie isna here?"

A young lass raised her hand.

"Speak."

She blanched, and he realized if he were to get any cooperation from this group so that supper would make it to the table, he lowered his voice. "Speak, lass."

"Margie never allowed anyone else to cook."

There were at least nine or ten workers in the room. "What do the rest of ye do, then?"

The brave young lass could no longer meet his eyes but studied the table. "Cut vegetables, cut meat, bring things to her while she cooks."

Haydon threw his hands up in the air, then left the kitchen. "Wife!"

Ainslee and her still weeping sister sat on a bench close to the fire in the great hall. Elsbeth looked as though she would swoon when he approached them.

"Haydon, you are scaring my sister."

He tried to soften his voice. "'Tis nothing to worry about, Elsbeth. I just chased Margie from the kitchen. She is no longer our cook."

The girl started weeping again.

Haydon threw his hands up in the air. "What now?"

"Who will cook?" Elsbeth said between sniffs.

"Ye and yer sister will cook until we can find another one." He waved his finger at them. "And a better cook 'twill be."

No' wishing to continue to listen to wails and sniffs, he turned on his heel and left the great hall. He stopped to look over his shoulder. "Ye better get into the kitchen since the evening meal is only a couple hours off."

* * *

AINSLEE WATCHED HER HUSBAND DEPART. She'd had every intention of replacing Margie with another, more skilled cook, but in time. Not in the middle of meal preparation. But then, Haydon had already laid down the law that he made the decisions. 'Twas too bad the person who made the decisions didn't get to handle the muddle he left behind.

Ainslee stood and pulled her sister up. "Cease yer tears. We have work to do."

Everything was silent in the kitchen. Ainslee looked around and wandered over to the large pot simmering over the fire. "What's this?"

No one answered.

If she and Elsbeth were to get supper ready in time, they needed the help of these workers, who all looked as if they were ready to bolt from the room.

"My sister and I will be taking o'er the cooking until we can find another cook. We would appreciate all yer help since we haven't done this before."

The kitchen maids all looked at each other.

Since that statement would not instill confidence in anyone, Ainslee decided a different tactic. She cleared her throat. "It appears Margie has started some sort of soup or stew, so we will let that be our supper. However, we will need bread—lots of it—and some sort of sweet afterward."

Frustrated with the lack of response, she pointed to a young girl slowly chopping carrots. "Who makes the bread?"

A young lad raised his hand. "I doona make the bread myself, but I've helped Margie make it a few times."

Ainslee let out a sigh of relief. "Verra good. Then get started. Make as many loaves as you normally do."

He nodded and left the room, most likely to gather the ingredients for the bread. Or to escape the keep. She'd have to watch the window to see if he raced from the building.

Having recovered from her upset, Elsbeth said, "Sister, I ken how to make a sweet pudding. Remember I used to make it for Da all the time?"

"Aye, ye did. Why doona ye make that, and I'll see if I can add something to this stew to make it taste better." She looked at another lass who was helping the lad load the peasemeal onto the table. "I believe Margie said ye dinna have an herb garden?"

"Aye. Once my lady passed away, Lady Donella dinna keep it up."

Ainslee nodded. "Do ye have any knowledge of gardening?"

The lass smiled. "Aye. I do. My mam has a huge garden. I helped her for years."

"Good," Ainslee said. "Ye are in charge of getting the herb garden back into use." She smiled at the lass. "Ye can start now. See if ye can save any of it."

The lass hurried from the kitchen.

Elsbeth had taken up preparing the sweet pudding. Ainslee wandered over to the table where the bread was being started. She examined the ingredients. "Why are you using peasemeal and pulsers? Doona we have flour? I would think a keep of this size and wealth could afford flour to at least be mixed with the other."

"Aye, we do, my lady, but Margie has it locked up."

"Indeed? And who has the key besides Margie?"

The girl shrugged. "No one, my lady. She carries it on her person all the time."

It appeared her young sister-in-law had really let things deteriorate since her mam's death. In fact, Ainslee had not seen the lass except for meals since she had married Haydon.

"Do ye ken where 'tis locked up?"

A young lad, another of the kitchen helpers, stood. "I ken where it is. She brought me there one time to help her unload it."

The two of them left the main floor and descended the stone steps to the underground area. 'Twas a dark and damp space and not a very good place to locate the granary. However, the reason for the choice of storage was made clear when they forced the door open with an axe the young lad brought with him from the kitchen.

The granary was empty.

They trooped back upstairs. Ainslee shoved her discovery to the back of her mind. Supper had to be served to hungry warriors, and she, Elsbeth, and the kitchen maids had a lot of work to do before it was ready.

Amazingly enough, hot bread, butter, and stew was placed on the tables less than one half hour after it was due. The meal was rounded out with Elsbeth's sweet pudding.

"'Twas a good job ye did, wife," Haydon said as he leaned back in his chair after finishing his supper.

"Thank ye, husband. When ye have time, I wish to speak with ye about the kitchen."

He waved at her. "'Tis yer responsibility, wife. I doona want to interfere with ye."

She felt the tightness starting in her stomach. "'Twas yer decision to remove Margie from the keep. Elsbeth and I worked hard to get supper on time. There are matters I can see in the kitchen that need to be changed."

"Verra well, then. Change them."

Before Ainslee could open her mouth, he added, "Just doona change anything without my permission."

Then the mon had the arrogance to lean close to her ear. "Eat up, wife. I would finish what we started before yer sister distracted us."

The anger just kept building. Now he wanted her to hurry through her meal so he could drag her upstairs for bed sport.

Malcolm approached the table. "My laird, a message has arrived from Glencairn."

Haydon stood and waved his cousin toward the door. "Gather the men who need to ken what's in the message. I will meet you in my solar."

Without saying a word to her, Haydon strode off, leaving her with a great deal of anger and nowhere to let it out.

After the trying day, a warm bath would be a fine way to soothe her. As she left the great hall, she stopped one of the maids. "Please have a bath sent up to the laird's bedchamber."

As she waited for the bath, she stood in the center of the bedchamber and smiled. Fresh linens and bed coverlet, along with the bed hangings recently beaten free of dust would certainly please her husband.

The rushes had been replaced, and herbs the young servant had found from the garden were scattered among the straw. The newly cleaned tapestries and window coverings had been put back up.

Ainslee removed her clothes and climbed into the tub. With the help of her maid, Gwyneth, she made quick work of it and was soon sitting in front of the fireplace, brushing her hair dry as she awaited Haydon.

After more than a couple of hours of fighting drowsiness, she climbed into the bed and fell into an exhausted sleep.

THE SUN WAS PEEKING under the window covers, a yellow stripe of light on the floor when she opened her eyes. 'Twas obviously past sunrise. She glanced over in the bed. Haydon's pillow didn't have an indentation, and the covers on his side had not been moved.

Where had her husband slept? And why did he 'order' her to finish up her meal so he could continue where they'd left off earlier if he didn't intend to join her?

Just then, Gwyneth entered the room. "Good morning, my lady. Ye were sleeping so soundly when I checked on ye before, I decided to let ye rest." She pulled the bed hangings over and moved to the window, drawing the covering aside.

She felt silly asking her lady's maid, but really had no choice. "Is the laird breaking his fast?"

"Nay." Gwyneth shook out a work gown she'd removed from the chest.

Well, he certainly had been up early from wherever he'd spent the night. She tried verra hard not to be concerned about that. She and Haydon had never discussed fidelity, and mayhaps she had been foolish enough to expect it.

Ainslee headed straight for the kitchen once she was dressed and ready for the day. Elsbeth was there, directing the servants in their jobs.

"Good morning, sister," Elsbeth said. "We thought ye would never rise."

"Is it truly that late?" Ainslee reached over and took an apple from the bowl on the worktable.

"Aye. 'Tis close to mid-morn I believe."

Just then, one of the warriors entered the kitchen. "Good morning, my lady." He reached for the bowl and grabbed a few apples, stuffing them into his pockets.

"Have ye seen the laird this morning?"

"Nay." He chewed a large chunk of the apple. "He's no' here."

Her brows rose at this news. "Where is he?"

The mon strolled out the back door. "He left last night for a meeting of the clans."

10

Haydon, Conall, and Malcom, along with an escort of about twenty warriors, arrived at Edinburgh in the early hours of the morning, having ridden through the night. The message Haydon had received hours before from William Cunningham, Earl of Glencairn, was to make their way as quickly as possible to Edinburgh.

Not sure why they were meeting there, Haydon was grateful for it, though since traveling to Dumfries, the home of Glencairn would have taken a few days instead of one.

They entered one of several inns in the overcrowded town, foregoing the couple hours of sleep they could have had and opted instead for a full breakfast to keep them awake.

Edinburgh was an interesting town. The walls surrounding the town kept new houses and buildings from being built. Therefore, with growth stymied, floors were added to already existing structures, giving the place an unkempt, dirty, overcrowded look.

"It appears there are several clan representatives here." Haydon nodded in the direction of other clan chiefs, Lords Huntly, MacDonald of Glengarry, and Seaforth, who entered right behind them and settled at a table on the other side of the room. The chiefs nodded to them and ordered ale from the young serving lass.

Several of their top warriors and aides filed in behind them, sitting at another table.

Haydon had heard rumors that although invited to join the rebellion, the Marquis of Argyll wished to remain on the sidelines, but his son, Lord Lorne, was making noises of wanting to defy his father and join. They were waiting to see what the son would do.

A hearty breakfast of sausages, eggs, bacon, black pudding, beans, tattie scones, fried tomatoes, mushrooms, and toast prepared them for the day. The sun was peeking over the horizon as they left the inn. After eating, they'd spent some time speaking with the other clans, but no one seemed to ken any more than they did as to why they'd been called for a meeting and why in Edinburgh.

They arrived at the designated meeting place, an old, falling down cottage in the middle of the woods on Scrymgeour land. John Scrymgeour, who had taken his father's place after he fell during the battle of Marston Moor, had commanded a regiment of royalists under the Duke of Hamilton. Haydon had no idea if Scrymgeour was joining their forces, but this was a somewhat safe place for the clans to meet.

Once they had all assembled, William sent a few of his

men to check the outside of the cottage. Once convinced no one lurked nearby, he addressed the group.

"The battle for our freedom is nearing." He slapped his fist into his hand. "'Tis time to drive the British back to where they belong and force them to leave us in peace. I need all of your firm commitments to the cause along with the number of soldiers I can count on."

The men all nodded their acceptance, and William continued. "However, the reason for this furtive meeting is to also inform you we have a spy among us."

The grumbling began as each mon looked around the room at the others. Haydon crossed his arms over his chest and leaned back. He had a knack for reading people, and he saw no one that looked to him as if they were hiding anything.

"What makes ye say that, Laird?" Haydon asked.

Cunningham focused on the question. "We have reason to believe there is someone working for the British with access to our information and strategy. When it came to my attention, I purposely put out false information, and it came back to me as fact."

"And ye cannot tell how it returned?"

The mon shook his head. "Nay. The person behind it had a web so entangled it would take weeks to work it out." He paused for a minute to look around the room. "'Tis sorry I am to bring ye so far from yer homes, but this is important. Before ye leave, I need a commitment from ye on soldiers, horses, and supplies. Coin too, if ye can spare it. Then I need ye to keep yer ears open for anything that sounds like deception."

"Do ye have any idea when we begin?" MacDonald asked.

"Nay. But the time grows near. Especially now that we ken there is a spy most likely reporting back to the bloody British."

They spent most of the day going over strategy, with each chieftain offering his warriors, horses, coin, and supplies.

Once they left the gathering, Haydon mounted Demon and turned to the other two men. "I'm all for returning to the inn and getting a room for the night. I doona think I could ride back again without some rest."

"How long did ye tell Ainslee ye would be gone?" Conall asked.

Haydon frowned. "I dinna tell my wife anything. The lass was upstairs in our bedchamber when we discussed the message from Cunningham and our trip here."

Conall stared at his brother. "So ye dinna even see the lass before ye left?"

Haydon glowered at Conall. "Isnae that what I just told ye? I dinna see my wife before I left." He waved his hand around. "Most likely she was asleep anyway."

He hated feeling guilty about Ainslee because he kenned his brother was right. He probably should have told her he was leaving. He soothed himself with the thought that even if he had told her, he wouldn't have kenned how long he would be gone, anyway.

"Ye probably hurt the lass's feelings," Malcolm tossed in.

Haydon growled his impatience. "Nay. The lass isnae soft. She kens as her laird, I doona have to explain to her or advise her of my comings and goings."

"Mayhaps not as her laird, but as her husband, ye might find things a bit different," Conall said.

"Enough! All this women's chatter is giving me a headache. Let's find a bed and eat a good meal. Tomorrow, at first light, we're off."

* * *

AINSLEE WIPED HER WET, sticky forehead with the back of her wet sticky wrist. Kitchen work was much harder than she'd realized. Right now, honey was everywhere. She'd dropped the small jug filled to the top, and she was still trying to clean up the mess.

The heat coming from the fireplace and the baking oven was making it difficult to even breathe.

"My lady, the meat is just about gone. I doona believe we have enough for even a soup." The young lass who'd helped her the first day in the kitchen, whose name was Bessie, looked in the large cauldron filled with vegetables and barley.

Ainslee sighed. Another shortage that she was beginning to believe Margie had been responsible for. There seemed to be no other explanation than the cook had been stealing from the keep kitchen. "I will speak with the laird when he returns to see where the rest of the meat is. I canno' believe Margie had a special place for it that she dinna let anyone else know about. When the laird returns, I shall have him go to her house and see what is what."

There were a lot of 'secret' places in the kitchen that only Margie kenned about. Trying to cook three meals for the warriors and the rest of the clan who ate in the great hall had been a challenge. She and Elsbeth had done their best, but the men were grumbling.

It had only been two days since Haydon had left. She

would surely beat the mon when he returned, leaving like that and not telling her where he was going or when he would return. And right after he fired the cook!

All she'd been able to learn was that he'd received a message, called a meeting with his aides, and left. No one kenned where he was headed.

"Hagen, the bread is burning!" Elsbeth rushed across the room and grabbed the long-handled paddle. Pushing the young lad aside, she began to remove the smoking loaves from the fire, dropping them onto the worktable.

"I'm sorry, my lady. I turned my back for only one minute, I assure you." Hagen helped her remove the loaves. Luckily only one or two appeared burned, although all of them were burned on the bottom since the bread oven was very difficult to clean out.

"My lady, we need your help." One of the young maids entered the kitchen.

"What is it, Alana?" Ainslee was still attempting to remove as much honey from her body and the worktable that she could.

"The men are all out on the list, and wee Donella needs help."

Of course, the lass would need help. She was certainly no help to her and Elsbeth.

"Is this something that can wait? We're trying to finish the supper so we're not too late this eve."

"Well, I think it might be a good idea to come see what she needs." The girl turned and hurried away. God's bones, all these clan members had a habit of rushing off without giving proper instructions.

So as not to lose her, Ainslee followed the girl out of

the kitchen and down the corridor past the great hall and out of the keep. "Where is Donella?"

"I will show ye." The girl continued, picking up her pace so Ainslee was forced to run to keep up with her.

They left the keep and the inner and outer bailey. What the devil was Donella doing outside the castle walls? Dinna she need permission from the laird to leave like Ainslee was told?

With a stitch in her side from running, and barely able to catch her breath, Ainslee almost crashed into Alana when the lass came to an abrupt stop. She bent over, taking in air. "Where is she?"

Alana pointed toward the sky. "Up there."

"I need help." The pathetic voice drew Ainslee's attention. High up on a branch in a very tall tree sat her sister-in-law, swinging her legs like a bairn.

Before even thinking, Ainslee shouted, "What the devil are you doing up there?"

Donella began to weep. "I was chased by a boar. I got scared and climbed the tree."

"Then climb back down."

"I cannae," she wailed.

Ainslee dropped her head into her hands, forgetting about the honey. She winced when her face met the sticky mess. She peeled her fingers away and looked up at Donella again. "'Tis not possible for me to carry a ladder from the keep to rescue you. Mayhaps I'll have to get one of the warriors to come."

"Nay!" Louder wailing. "Haydon will be most upset if I disturb the men's training."

God's bones, the girl was a trial. Having no other solution, she bent, reached between her legs and drew her skirts up, tucking them into her belt. She turned to Alana. "You may return to yer duties."

The lass scurried away.

Ainslee looked at the tree again and could see an easy path to the lass. "Hold on, Donella, I'm coming up for ye."

* * *

THE MEN and their escorts arrived at the castle right before the evening meal. Haydon desired a wash, to rid himself of the road dirt, but after stewing most of the way home on his brother's words, he thought it best to find his wife first.

He headed directly to the kitchen. There was a great deal of activity, but Ainslee was nowhere in sight. He walked over to Elsbeth, who was cutting burnt pieces of crust off bread. "Where is Ainslee?"

"I'm not sure, laird. I left the kitchen to fetch some of the few herbs left in the garden, and when I came back, she was gone."

He looked at the other servants. "Do any of ye ken where your mistress is?"

"I believe she went off with Alana."

Mayhaps there was a problem in one of the rooms the servants were working on. He headed up the stairs to the bedchamber floor. She wasn't in any of the rooms, and no one kenned where she was.

An unfamiliar feeling of fear for the lass gripped him. Certainly, his wife wouldn't disobey his orders and leave the castle again?

A search of the entire keep, both baileys, and the stables dinna turn up his elusive wife.

He glanced out the window, noting the sun was beginning its descent. Soon, it would be dark, and the fear returned full force. Although he'd forbidden it, he had to assume she'd left the castle again.

"Are ye looking for yer wife, Laird?" One of his guardsmen shouted from the top of the wall.

Haydon blocked the setting sun with his hand. "Aye. Have ye seen her?"

"She and one of the lasses left a while ago."

He placed his hands on his hips. "And ye dinna stop her?"

The guard shrugged. "I dinna ken she wasn't allowed to leave."

He would deal with that nonsense posthaste, but now, he wanted to find the woman. "Did she say where she was headed?"

"Nay. They were both running in the direction of the woods."

He would kiss the life out of her when he found her for causing him distress. Then he would throttle her and lock her in their bedchamber for a month.

Was the lass so feebleminded then, that she didn't understand the danger? Or so stubborn about obeying his orders that she risked being hurt or killed to defy him?

He sprinted away from the castle and entered the woods. All was quiet and slowly growing dark. His heart thundered at the silence, afraid she and whoever it was that had accompanied her had met with trouble. With the talk at the meeting about spies, the danger to everyone involved in the potential rebellion was high.

Anyone wishing to manipulate him would do so by using his wife. Damn his growing feelings for the lass. He needed to get himself under control. He never intended to have a wife that would be more than someone to run the keep and provide heirs. He'd been trying his best to keep a distance between them, but now with her missing, he realized there was no distance great enough for him not to be swallowed by pain should something happen to her.

Desperate for some response, he called out her name.
Silence.
He walked farther into the woods and called again.
Silence.

With it growing darker by the minute, he refused to give up. He tried one more time and heard a faint, "Haydon."

He ran toward the voice. "Ainslee? Call again so I can find ye."

Her voice was stronger now, until she was clear as a bell, but he dinna see her. "Where are ye, lass?" Had she been attacked and was lying somewhere tied up?

"Up here."
"Up where?"
A loud sigh. "Look up, Haydon."

In the shadows of the increasing darkness, he saw his wife and another lass sitting on a branch in the tree above him.

"What in God's name are ye doing up there in the tree?" He felt as though his chest would explode. Was there no end to the vexation the lass would cause him? "And who is the other senseless lass up there with ye?"

A soft voice answered. "'Tis me, Haydon. Yer sister, Donella." Then she burst into tears.

11

Haydon let out with a stream of curses that would have Ainslee saying prayers for the arrogant oaf's soul for weeks.

"Do ye think ye might help us down from here before it's too dark to see anything?" She was tired of sitting in the tree. She'd climbed up, thinking to help Donella down, but learned too late 'twas a much scarier way down than up. Also, the boar had returned a few times to sniff around the base of the tree as if to remind them he awaited their descent.

The air had grown chilly, and all she wanted to do was leave the damn tree and go to her bedchamber. The last thing she was interested in was listening to Haydon lecture her all the way back to the keep. Especially after *he'd* disappeared without a word to her. She was still angry at him for that.

Haydon's voice interrupted her thoughts. "The only way for ye to leave the tree is to drop to the ground."

"Nay, 'tis a long drop. Ye also need to be careful of the boar that chased yer sister up the tree to begin with."

"Ach, lass, you certainly try my patience. I hope the boar does return, 'twill make a fine kill for the table." He paused for a moment. "Ye will have Donella drop first, and I will catch her. Then ye drop, and I'll catch ye."

It was most likely the only way for them to leave their perch. She turned to her sister-in-law. "Ye heard yer brother. Ye drop first."

The lass began to wail again. "I cannae. I'll break my neck."

"Nay," Ainslee said. "Haydon will catch ye."

When the lass continued to shake her head, Ainslee quelled the urge to pull the lass free of the branch she clung to and toss her to the ground. "Donella, ye must be reasonable. Haydon will not let ye get hurt. Doona ye trust yer own brother?"

Donella didn't answer, but kept staring at the ground, which was almost invisible by this time.

"Donella, this is yer laird speaking," Haydon bellowed, "and I am giving ye an order. Have Ainslee help ye hang from the branch yer sitting on. 'Twill put ye closer to the ground. Then just let go, and I will catch ye."

After many tears and protests, the lass moved into position. She looked up at Ainslee. "I cannae let go."

Completely out of patience, Ainslee pried her sister-in-law's fingers from the branch. Donella screamed, which ended in an oof sound when she landed in Haydon's arms.

"Yer next, lass."

She was so eager to leave the tree she would have

jumped headfirst at that point. She wiggled herself around, then hung by her sticky fingers. "I'm dropping."

"I'm here, lass. Just let go."

She landed in Haydon's warm, strong arms. She felt safe for the first time in hours. Then she looked at his face in the very dim light and thought perhaps returning to the tree branch might be a good idea.

He placed her on her feet. She rearranged her skirts and followed him back to the keep. She had to run almost as fast as she did when she followed Alana. But since the air was quite cold by then, she didn't mind.

When they arrived at the keep, the evening meal was well underway. All she wanted to do was warm up. Perhaps guessing her intention, Haydon took her elbow. "Eat yer meal, wife. Then ye can get a warm bath."

"I must clean my hands first; they are sticky with honey."

Her husband apparently didn't care to hear the story of how that had come about, so he pointed to the kitchen. "Get yourself cleaned up then."

She gritted her teeth, ready to hit him in the head with the nearest cup of ale. Instead, she stormed off to the kitchen and scrubbed her hands so hard they turned red.

Haydon glowered at her when she returned. She raised her chin in the air and took the seat alongside him. One of the serving girls was laying down trenchers of food in front of her and Haydon.

Without speaking to each other, they ate their meal. By the time it had ended, Ainslee felt as though she would fall asleep right there at the table.

"Go on upstairs, lass. Ye need a bath to warm up. I'll join ye in a little while."

Another order. She was truly growing weary of his commands. She was not one of his soldiers, and she would let him ken that as soon as the mon joined her.

In the meantime, she would enjoy a nice warm bath.

Once she had soaked for a while, enjoying Gwyneth washing her hair, she climbed out of the tub and wrapped her refreshed body in a soft linen. She sat in front of the fire to dry her hair.

Gwyneth was only gone for a short while when the door to the bedchamber slammed open. Her husband stood in the entryway, glaring at her again.

She sighed. "Please, my laird. I am no' in the mood for another lecture. 'Tis been a long day, and I only wish to rest."

He stood in front of her, his arms crossed over his chest, his feet spread apart. "I would have a word with ye first."

"Of course ye would." She hopped up and pushed her finger into his chest. "Mayhap I want a word with ye as well."

His eyes widened. "I am yer laird. I speak first, then if I wish, I grant ye permission to speak."

"I disagree."

He waved her off and began to undress. "No matter."

"Ach!" She stomped across the room, climbed into the bed, and immediately turned her back on the arrogant oaf. She punched her pillow several times, wishing it was his head.

The bed dipped as he joined her. She immediately felt the heat from his warm naked body radiating toward her. Despite her anger, she edged closer to him since there was a chill in the room.

Haydon wrapped his arm around her and drew her next to him, so her back was flush against his chest. "Lass, ye scared me to death, ye ken?"

She turned and faced him. "Why?"

He smoothed her still damp hair away from her face. "Because ye disappeared. No one kenned where you were. I searched the entire castle and then find out ye went outside the walls again when I ordered ye not to do it." His voice rose as he continued his rant. "Ye are smart enough to ken how dangerous the times are. Ye can't go wandering around the woods climbing trees like a bairn."

She attempted to hold her temper. It was obvious from his expression as well as his words that he'd been worried about her. As happy as she was to ken he cared, she chaffed at the knowledge that he thought her foolish enough to abandon her duties in the middle of preparing the evening meal to leave the castle and climb a tree.

Taking a deep breath, not wishing to escalate this into an argument when she had much more important things to discuss, she said, "I dinna go outside the walls to climb a tree, husband. Alana came to me in the kitchen telling me that yer sister needed help. She dinna say what the problem was, and I followed her. She led me outside the walls into the woods."

"Dinna ye think perhaps she wanted ye to leave the protection of the castle and used that excuse to lure ye away?"

"Alana's one of our servants!"

Haydon pulled her closer until she felt the strong beat of his heart against her breasts.

"Lass, the meeting I attended was for the upcoming rebellion that William Cunningham is planning. We learned at that meeting that there is a spy working for the bloody British. The spy could be anywhere."

It seemed hard for her to believe the young lass was a spy, but she did understand Haydon's worry when he returned from the meeting and found her missing. Maybe for once, he was right and she shouldn't argue the point with him.

"Aye, I understand yer concern, but I couldno' leave yer sister sitting in a tree until ye returned." She poked him in the chest again. "And that is what I wish to speak with ye about."

* * *

HAYDON HAD STILL NOT RECOVERED from the fright his wife had given him when she was missing. The plan for an uprising and now the concern of a spy in one of the castles, times were becoming increasingly dangerous. He wanted to wrap her up in his plaid and leave her in the bedchamber so she would ne'er get into trouble.

This was definitely not what he had in mind when he approached the Johnstone about marrying one of his daughters. He'd wanted a meek, submissive wife who he could place in his castle and mostly ignore, except when it came to producing heirs. One who would obey his every order without question or argument.

"What is it ye wish to discuss, lass?"

She shifted around until she rested on her elbows and looked right into his eyes as if she had every right to chastise him. If it would not encourage her to think she could lecture him, he would laugh at her daring.

He, however, could not think about anything except

her warm, lush body covered by the thin nightdress she wore. He reached out and began to untie the tiny ribbon holding the top of the garment together.

She swatted his hand. "Stop. This is serious."

He took a deep breath and nodded. "Aye."

"I am yer wife."

"Did ye stop what I was having such a good time doing to tell me something I've kenned for a while now?"

She had the nerve to wave her finger at him. "Doona interrupt."

He took in a deep breath. "Lass, yer getting into trouble here. You doona tell your laird not to speak."

"Nay. I dinna tell my laird, I told my husband."

God, he loved how her eyes flashed when she was angry. Also, when she was feeling passion, which brought him right back to where he had planned to be when he'd entered the bed. He rolled over onto his back and placed his linked fingers under his head. With a deep sigh, he said, "Continue, wife."

"Ye should not leave the castle for a lengthy trip without telling me."

"Nay."

"What does that mean?"

"It means I am the laird. I doona account to anyone for my time."

Ainslee jumped from the bed, yanking the bottom of her nightdress that had been caught under Haydon's leg. "I believe I will sleep in the chamber next to this one."

He reached out and grabbed her hand, pulling her back. She was powerless to stop him as she tumbled and landed in the spot she'd just left.

"I dinna give ye permission to leave."

She opened her mouth, no doubt to dispute him when he drew her flush against him and covered her mouth with his. She held herself stiff for all of about ten seconds and then melted against him.

He pulled back and whispered against her lips. "Let's get rid of this nightdress."

When it appeared she wanted to continue their discussion, he covered her breast with his hand and massaged, plucking on the nipple until she gave a soft moan.

That was all the invitation he needed to reach down and pull her nightdress off. Her warm, soft body ignited a fire in him so strong it was almost crippling. "Lass, ye do such things to me. I want to hold ye and love ye throughout the night."

Her small hands roamed his body, her fingers tugging lightly on the hairs on his chest as he once more returned to her mouth, nudging her lips until she opened. "Sweet. So verra sweet."

He gripped her hair and tilted her head allowing him to go deeper with the kiss as he rolled over her, his heart pounding. He had no idea how long he could control himself, he wanted her so much. If the lass only kenned how important she had become to him, he would lose a great deal of control.

"Ach, Haydon, I need ye to help me."

"Aye, *mo chridhe*, I will never leave ye unsatisfied." He moved his hand down to use his thumb to brush over the sensitive nerves at her opening. She began to pant and shift her legs around.

"Aye. That."

She opened her eyes, staring up at him and licked her lips. He almost came undone. It was too easy to get lost in the way she looked at him. Lowering his head, he drew her lush breast into his mouth and suckled. With a loud groan, Ainslee came apart in his arms, moaning his name over and over.

That was all he needed to quickly shift his body and thrust himself inside her warm moistness. He could still feel the waves of her release as he entered. "Aye, lass. Ye feel too good."

He kenned he wasn't going to last. "'Tis sorry I am, but I want ye so much I cannot hold back." With those words he thrust a few more times and then poured his seed into her.

After a few moments, he moved off her, pulling her close to his side. It took a bit of time for their breathing to return to normal. She traced circles on his chest with her finger while he ran his hand lightly up and down her back. When she shivered at his side, he reached down and pulled the cover over them.

Within minutes they were both sound asleep.

12

*A*inslee rolled over in the soft, warm bed and moved her hand to the space next to her.

Empty. And cold.

She sat up and pushed her hair over her shoulders and frowned at the vacant place where her husband's body should be. The mon had managed to escape before she had the rest of her say about him leaving without telling her. The night before, he had distracted her, and although she'd found it quite enjoyable, she still wanted to get the matter of him leaving without saying goodbye straightened out.

Gwyneth knocked lightly on the door and entered. "Good morning, my lady." She went around moving the window covers aside and tugging on the bed hangings. "Did ye sleep well?"

"Aye. But I need to hurry, there is a lot to be done, and I must catch my husband before he is off for the day." She stopped as she walked to the wash bowl. "Do ye ken if he is still here? Or has he already left?"

"I just saw him in the great hall before I came up here. He was breaking his fast, so he will most likely be there for a while."

"Thank ye." She finished washing, and with Gwyneth's help, she quickly dressed, opting for a braid hanging down her back instead of having the maid fuss with her hair.

Haydon was indeed still in the great hall when she entered. She took the seat next to him and reached for an apple and a chunk of cheese. One of the serving lasses poured ale into a cup and placed it in front of her.

"Husband, I would speak with ye before ye are off for the day."

Haydon grinned at her. "Well, my lady, ye will be pleased to ken that I will be at yer side all day."

Her eyes grew wide. "'Tis true?"

"Aye. Elsbeth spoke with me this morn and mentioned the missing supplies from the kitchen. I also want to make a trip into the village to visit with some of the clansmen."

"I would go too?"

"Aye."

She immediately pushed aside continuing their conversation about him leaving the keep without telling her. If she was to have his help in dealing with the kitchen and then make a trip into the village, she dinna want to spoil it all by resuming the argument.

Before when she'd gone to the village by herself, she found everyone to be friendly, and even more so when she mentioned she was the laird's new wife. But to have Haydon by her side when they met the clansfolk would be better.

"Elsbeth wasn't too clear on what the problems were in

the kitchen. She fidgeted and never looked me in the eye. She then suggested I speak with ye."

Ainslee grinned. "She's afraid of ye."

"Who?"

"Elsbeth. Ye frighten her, ye big oaf."

He leaned forward and whispered in her ear. "I doona frighten ye, though?"

"Nay." She smiled. "I'm afraid of no mon."

Haydon drew back and immediately lost his pleasant demeanor. "Doona say that lass. Ye doona seem able to get into yer head that 'tis dangerous beyond these walls. Ye should be afraid of any other mon except me."

"Even yer brother?"

He rolled his eyes. "Nay. If ye find yerself in trouble ye can always call on Conall."

She finished up her cheese and apple and gulped down the rest of the ale. "Come into the kitchen, and I will show ye what the problems have been."

Ainslee recited a litany of all the issues they'd discovered since Margie left. She brought him to the empty granary and then to the other underground room where the meat was stored. Or would have been stored had there been any. The little that was found after Margie had left had already been used.

Haydon glared at the empty room. "It appears there's been some pilfering going on."

"Aye. That's why the meals have been so scarce of meat."

He placed his hand on her back and moved her forward. "Come, we must fix this before we have our own uprising. The men train hard all day, they're no' happy with no meat."

"We also need a new cook," Ainslee said as they climbed the damp stone steps back up to the kitchen. "Elsbeth and I are trying our best, but we dinna do much cooking before now."

"Aye, from what I've heard from the men 'tis obvious."

Ainslee drew in a breath, her temper flaring. "Seeing as how ye fired the cook and then took off without a word to anyone, 'tis a miracle the men got a meal at all."

If she'd expected Haydon to look remorseful, she was in for a disappointment. Her husband merely shrugged as they entered the kitchen once again.

With rapid instructions, first Haydon had Hagen, the young lad who baked the bread fetch Malcolm from the lists. Then he turned to the other kitchen maids in the room. "Which of ye can cook?"

When no one answered, he said, "Do ye ken of anyone who can take over the cooking?"

Bessie raised her hand. "My mam is a fine cook, Laird. Since Da passed away, we've been struggling. My wages doona cover much."

He nodded. "First off, if yer mam is having problems, she should have come to me. Next, since ye look well fed to me, I think your mam might be the answer. Go bring her back here."

The lass hurried away just as Malcolm arrived at a run. "Yes, Laird. What do you need?"

"I want ye to take half the men and have them hunt. There's plenty of game out there in the woods, as well as at least one wild boar." He turned and winked at Ainslee.

"Have the other half head to the shore and pull in some fish. We must restore our larders. Were we attacked today we would all starve in less than two days."

Ainslee was amazed and a bit annoyed. Why hadn't she thought of asking the other servants if they kenned someone who could cook? Or consider asking the men to hunt?

Elsbeth entered the kitchen holding bunches of herbs she'd managed to salvage from the garden.

Haydon turned to her. "Lass, yer job is to get that garden producing again. Also, check the vegetable garden to see that it's also taken care of."

Elsbeth looked confused, most likely at Haydon's abruptness. She dropped the pile of herbs onto the worktable. Ainslee looked over at Alana. "Wash and sort these, then hang them up to dry."

Her sister hastened from the kitchen.

"Husband, another problem is the bread. The baking oven needs a good cleaning. All the breads are burnt on the bottom. I must admit I have no idea how to clean the thing."

Haydon nodded. "We need bread. I'll grab one of the men headed to the woods and have him and a few others move the oven outside and then figure out how to clean it."

"What about all their training?" Ainslee asked.

"One day will not interfere. I expect the larder to be stocked by the end of the day."

With that order from the laird, people began to scatter. She'd never seen the kitchen so lively. Before she could comment on that, Haydon reached out. "Let us go, lass. We have much to do ourselves."

The whirlwind continued as Haydon hustled her out of the keep and around to the stables. Both horses were awaiting them, her husband obviously having given the order for the horses to be tacked before she'd arrived from their bedchamber.

With a flick of his wrist, it seemed, he encircled her waist with his large hands and plopped her onto her horse.

"My goodness, husband. I barely have time to catch my breath."

"We need to be on our way. Ye can breathe later." With those words, they took off, the keep falling far behind them as they raced toward the village.

About a mile before they were to enter the village square, Haydon veered off the path and continued in an easterly direction. After about ten minutes they arrived at a small cottage.

Haydon jumped from his horse. "Stay here, lass. This won't take long." He knocked a few times, but no one opened the door. Haydon walked around the cottage and looked in the windows. Shaking his head, he returned to his horse.

"Whose cottage is this?"

"Margie. But it appears she's long gone. I'm sure with the coin she managed to steal from me, she's headed to Inverness or Edinburgh so she canno' be caught."

They backtracked and continued to the village. When Ainslee had been there before, she didn't get to see much. She'd grown thirsty almost as soon as she spotted the inn where Haydon had found her.

Now as she looked around, she was quite pleased. Many small shops formed a rectangle around the village green. She spotted a carpenter, a bakery, and a butcher, along with the usual blacksmith, fletcher, potter, and cooper.

The shops seemed to have drawn quite a few shoppers. 'Twas a bustling place, and it brought a smile to her face to see all the activity.

"Does the castle host a market day?" Ainslee asked once their horses had been stabled and they strolled along amidst the crofters.

"Aye. Usually once a month those who travel from castle to castle come to Dornoch." He smiled at her. "I remember buying ye a ribbon at the marketplace at Lochwood Tower when we visited yer da's keep."

"Aye. 'Twas a pretty ribbon."

Haydon leaned in close to her ear. "A pretty ribbon for a bonnie lass."

Despite having shared a bed with the mon, she still found Haydon to be a puzzle. He was arrogant, cold at times, and demanding. Yet there was a side of him only she saw. A side that peeled away her defenses. She dinna want to fall in love with the mon and become one of those wives who said 'aye' to every command. 'Twas not in her future.

"Good morn, Laird." An older mon, bent over from years of hard labor approached them. "Is this yer bonnie new bride? I heard tales of her."

"Aye, Thomas. Lady Sutherland and I are taking a wee stroll through the village." He rested his hand on the older man's shoulder. "And how do ye fare? Is yer son taking good care of yer land?"

"Aye, Laird. William is a good lad. He and his bonnie wife, Madeline, have four bairns now." He stuck his chest out. "All sons. They will one day all be strapping men."

"Glad to hear it, Thomas. Tell Madeline and William I send my good wishes."

Ainslee smiled at the mon. "'Tis a pleasure to meet ye, Thomas. Even though we've ne'er met, send my regards to yer son and his family, as well."

The mon actually blushed, which amused Ainslee, but she kept her expression bland, lest she embarrass the mon.

They continued their stroll, stopping at a few tables in the center of the village green that held items not sold in the shops. The smell of scones filled the air, and Ainslee's stomach immediately rumbled.

Haydon looked down at her with raised brows. "It sounds to me, lass, that yer needing a bit of food."

She nodded. "Aye. The apple and cheese weren't enough. Those scones smell wonderful." She left his side and walked to where a rotund woman was passing out warm scones. "Are these from the bakery?" Ainslee asked.

"Aye, my lady. Fresh from the oven."

"Wonderful. I would have one, please."

Before the woman passed the scone to her, Haydon said behind her back, "Make that a few scones, Freya."

"Good morn, Laird. 'Tis a fine day for ye to be strolling around." She nodded in Ainslee's direction. "I heard ye took a bonnie wife, and I assume this is Lady Sutherland?"

"Aye—" Haydon began when Ainslee interrupted him.

"I am pleased to meet you, Freya. Your scones smell delicious, and my stomach would not allow me to pass you by."

The woman's smile covered her face, her red cheeks growing redder at the compliment. She dipped a slight curtsey. "Thank ye, my lady." She handed four scones to Haydon who dropped a few coins into her hand.

Once they were a few steps away, Ainslee said, "I would like to speak with yer people, as well, Haydon."

"So it appeared. However, do not interrupt me when I am speaking."

Instead of growing angry, Ainslee rolled her eyes and bit into her scone. "More orders, Laird?"

"Aye."

They spent a pleasant couple of hours strolling along, visiting with the vendors and crofters and stopping in some of the shops. Even though Haydon had ordered her not to interrupt him, he did introduce her first, then stepped back, allowing her to speak with the villagers.

Aye, the mon was a puzzle.

As they neared the inn, she glanced around the area and took in a deep breath. "Haydon, you must stop that."

He looked where she was pointing. A very large, very angry mon was beating a young lad. The bairn was trying to escape his da's wrath, but the mon held tight. The wails of the little one carried to Ainslee.

They both hurried to the mon. "Stop that, Patrick!" Haydon pushed the mon's shoulder so he reeled back. When he fell to the ground and had some difficulty rising, it was apparent he had been drinking quite a bit.

The lad ran right into Ainslee's arms, sobbing. He looked to be no more than four summers. He shook against her, hiding his face in her skirts. She knelt and looked at the lad. His face and thin arms were covered in bruises, some new, some old.

She stood and glared at the mon just as he was climbing to his feet. "Ye doona deserve to have a fine lad such as this." She pulled the child behind her.

Haydon placed his hands on his hips and studied the

mon. "Patrick, I told ye before to keep yer fists to yerself. No mon with the Sutherland name should ever put his hands on someone weaker than him and who is under his protection."

"The lad is stupid!" The words came out garbled. "He cannae do anything I order him to do." He wiped the spittle that spewed from his mouth.

Ainslee raised her chin and directed her comments to her husband. "My laird, I am bringing this lad home with us. He needs his bruises looked at." With those words, she scooped the much-too-light lad into her arms. With an abrupt turn, she headed toward the village stables where their horses were.

Several people nodded and smiled at her as she passed by. Before she reached the stables, Haydon had joined her. "How bad is the lad?"

Ainslee shook her head. "I willnae ken until I get a good look at him. But, Haydon, that mon could have killed him!"

"Aye. I've had problems with him before."

"Where is the lad's mother?"

They stood in the now cooling air while the stable-master readied their horses. The lad had fallen asleep in her arms, his small head resting on her shoulder.

"Emma died o'er a year ago."

"Did he beat her, too?"

"Aye. I even locked him up in the dungeon after one beating that almost took the lass's life."

"Are there sisters and brothers?"

"Nay. Emma bore two more bairns, but neither lived past one summer."

She handed the lad to Haydon, and with the stablemaster's help, she climbed onto her horse. She reached down to take the child from him. By the time he was settled in her lap, with her plaid wrapped around him, Haydon had mounted Demon.

As the horse started up, the lad awoke and began crying and pointing behind them. At first, Ainslee thought the da had come after them, but when she turned, she saw a small limping dog approaching the horses. The lad kept pointing and wailing, "*Mo chu!*"

The dog continued to bark as the lad cried. She looked at the tiny body in her arms. "Is that yer dog?"

"Aye."

She turned to Haydon. "We cannae leave the poor animal here. He looks as though he's gotten a beating himself."

Haydon shook his head, then shrugged. He vaulted from Demon, grabbed the small animal, then climbed back up, the dog tucked snugly in his lap.

"'Tis been an interesting day at the village, my lady."

13

Haydon had intended to bring the dog to the kitchen and let the servants take care of it. However, once Ainslee started up the stairs with the lad in her arms he began to cry again and reached for his dog.

"Haydon, please. Let the dog come upstairs with the lad. At least until he feels comfortable."

Haydon was beginning to feel as though he was losing control. Not that he regretted saving the lad from his da's wrath, but now it seemed Ainslee was making decisions and giving him orders.

That would not continue. He was following her around like the puppy in his arms. The lass was making him soft.

She looked at him over her shoulder. "I will bring him to the nursery on the floor above."

He frowned. "How did ye ken where the nursery was?"

"I went through the entire castle to see what shape everything was in, remember?" She continued up the stairs. "And I was left alone—without notice, I might add

—a mere couple of weeks after I gained a husband who dinna feel the need to let me know he was leaving."

He'd had enough. "Be verra careful, Ainslee," he growled. "I doona allow criticism."

She nudged the door open with her hip. "And why is that, Laird? Because ye are perfect?"

He stabbed his chest with his thumb, his anger growing. "Because I am the laird, and I give the orders. I dinna allow any back talking."

She tossed back the bedcover. "From yer soldiers."

His jaw tightened. "From everyone in my clan."

Ainslee laid the lad down on the soft bed. The poor bairn looked back and forth between them with wide eyes.

His wife sat alongside the lad and smoothed his hair back from his forehead. "Haydon, I believe we should cease. I think we are scaring the lad."

No doubt the poor child had seen many fights between his parents, and dinna need to witness any more anger from them. "Ye are right, lass." He paused and pointed a finger at her. "Dinna take that as surrender on my part."

She dipped her head. "Can I ask ye to have one of the servants fetch a pan of hot water, soap, some clean linens, and my medicament satchel from our bedchamber?"

"Aye." He strode from the nursery, still tense over their discussion. He'd kenned when Ainslee had switched places with her sister at their wedding that his life would not be one of peaceful submission on the part of his wife as he had planned when he offered for Elsbeth. But the lass needed to understand he would accept no criticism and no disobeying his orders.

He was her husband, laird, and protector. What he thought was best for her was the way it would be.

He had Alana fetch the supplies Ainslee had asked for, and then took notice of the new cook busy giving orders to the servants occupied with various chores at the worktables. The baking oven had been moved from the kitchen for cleaning. He was satisfied at how well things were improving.

He approached her. "Good day, Jonet. I am grateful that ye agreed to take over cooking for the castle."

She wiped the sweat from her forehead with the back of her wrist. "Thank ye, my laird. I appreciate the chance to help ye out."

Leaning closer to her, he said, "Yer daughter Bessie told me ye are having some difficult times since Alec died."

The woman's shoulders slumped. "Aye, it has been a bit troubling, but my lass should not have bothered ye with that."

He held up his hand to stop her. "Nay, Jonet. I am yer laird. 'Tis my job to take care of my clan. If ye have troubles, they become my troubles, ye ken?"

She touched the edge of her apron to her eyes. "Ye are the best, my laird."

He waited until she composed herself. "How many bairns have ye? And how many years?"

"Besides Bessie, I have five. Angus has seen twelve summers, Arabella eleven, the twins Callum and Camden eight, and my little lass, Catte four."

He nodded. "Send Angus to the stablemaster, and I'll tell him to give the lad a job. Now before ye object, old Broderick needs the help, but he's too proud to ask for it."

Jonet patted her eyes again. "Thank ye, Laird. With me working and now Angus, along with Bessie, we will be fine." Her beaming smile was all he needed to remind himself how important it was for him to do his duty.

After Alana had gathered all the things Ainslee had required to tend to the lad, Haydon gave some thought to Donal's thin little body. Certainly, a good hearty meal for the lad would not go amiss.

Once he loaded up a tray with cheese, warm bread, a bit of cold meat left from the night before, and a large cup of milk with a drop of honey, he headed upstairs. He also wanted to see how much damage the lad had suffered. He would take Patrick to task over this.

Ainslee had the boy stripped down to his skin. Haydon put the tray down and sucked in a breath at the bruises on the lad's body. When he saw a drop of water fall to his little chest, he looked at Ainslee to see her wiping away tears.

"This is unspeakable, Haydon." She turned and looked at him. "Do you see the damage his poor body has gone through? Patrick should be chained up and whipped."

"Nay, my lady," the lad wailed. "Doona do anything to Da, or he will hit me again." The dog—not too clean—had climbed up onto the bed and was cuddled in Donal's arms. The lad stroked the animal, which seemed to have a calming effect on him.

She cupped his cheek in her hand. "Doona worry, Donal, yer da will never get his hands on ye again."

"Ye shouldn't be promising the lad that, Ainslee." Haydon had planned to speak with Patrick and possibly throw him into the dungeon again, but the child would have to be returned to his da at some point.

Ainslee stopped wiping the dirt from the lad's body and turned to him. "Donal will not leave this castle."

"Ever?"

"Aye. Patrick will not raise his fists to the lad as long as I have breath in my body."

Ach. It appeared they were headed to another argument. Rather than disturb the lad once more, he placed the tray of food at the foot of the bed. The child eyed it with wide eyes and licked his lips.

He smiled at the look on the lad's face. "Once Lady Sutherland finishes, Donal, ye will have all the food on this tray."

"Aye, my laird? All of it. Just for me?"

Haydon's stomach twisted. "Aye lad, just for ye."

He walked to where Ainslee was now applying salve to cuts on the lad's chest. "How does he fare?"

She shook her head. "Not well. Fortunately, nothing seems broken, but ye can see the cuts and bruises on his wee body." She inhaled deeply, a shuddering sound, then turned to him. "How can anyone do this to a bairn? And one of yer own?" The anger in her eyes was fierce.

Unfortunately, Haydon had no answer for her. He would never treat an innocent bairn like that. God's bones, he would never raise his fist to anyone weaker than him. 'Twas a promise he'd made before God to protect his wife and any bairns they might have. Teach them, care for them, make sure they were all well-fed and warm.

It took about another ten minutes of work, with Donal eyeing the tray the entire time. Eventually, Ainslee stood, wiping her fingers on one of the cloths. "That is what I can do for now, Donal. I want ye to stay in bed for a couple of days. Just eat and rest."

Had it not been such a serious situation, the shock on the little boy's face would have been comical. "Aye? What about my work?"

Ainslee sat back down next to the lad and took his tiny hand in hers. "No work until yer better, ye ken?" When he grinned, she said, "Aye. Now eat yer food."

Twice, Ainslee had to remind him to chew his food and to not eat so fast. It was apparent the lad had been starved for some time. She watched every bite he put into his mouth, her smile growing as he ate.

While consuming his meal, she asked questions. "How many summers have ye seen, Donal?"

"Six."

Haydon and Ainslee looked at each other in shock. With the size of him, the lad had certainly not gotten proper food for a long time. Mayhaps, even before Emma died, which meant to him that Emma's death may not have been the ague Patrick had claimed it to be. Could it have been the poor woman had starved to death, saving whatever food she was able to get to give to her bairn?

He was beginning to think that perhaps Ainslee had the right of it, and the lad should not be returned to his da. But that was something for him to decide, not his wife.

Once the last bite of food had been swallowed, and some of the cold meat sneaked to the dog, wee Donal's eyes grew heavy. Ainslee gathered the tray and handed it to Haydon. She turned to the lad. "I want ye to sleep. Yer body needs to heal, and food and sleep are the best things for that, ye ken?"

"Aye, my lady." He let out with a huge yawn.

Ainslee bent and kissed Donal on the forehead. "Sleep, wee one. I will be back to check on ye in a little while."

He cuddled close to the wee dog and closed his eyes. Before they shut the door, the lad was asleep.

Ainslee hurried down the stairs to the floor where their bedchamber was. He expected her to continue down to the main floor, either to the great hall or the kitchen, but she made her way to their bedchamber instead.

Curious, he followed her. He stopped one of the servants and handed her the tray with the empty bowl and dirty linens. "Please return this to the kitchen."

"Aye, my laird."

Ainslee's medicament bag swayed back and forth as she strode down the corridor to the bedchamber, then opened the door.

When he entered the room, he found his wife sitting on their bed, her hands covering her face, weeping. His plan to lecture her on her behavior flew out the window at the sight. She was genuinely distraught.

With a deep sigh, he crossed the room and sat alongside her. Placing his arm around her shoulders, he pulled her to his chest. She turned and rested her head on his shoulder. "That wee lad has seen so much pain and horror in his short life." She sat up and wiped her eyes. "I want ye to go over to that mon right now and kill him. Slowly. And painfully."

He tried very hard not to laugh at such an outrageous statement. But he kenned Ainslee was not in the mood for humor. He pushed back the hair from her face that had fallen from her braid. "'Tis a sad situation, I agree."

She jumped from the bed and began to pace. "How can ye allow this to happen?" Before he could open his mouth, she continued. "Ye said the mon had already been thrown in the dungeon for beating his wife. He should have stayed there until he rotted."

"Calm yerself, wife."

"Nay!" She fisted her hands on her hips. "I shall not calm down until ye promise me the lad will stay here."

"I cannae just keep a mon's child."

She waved her hands around, her face flushed. "Aye, ye can. Ye tell me all the time ye are the laird and ye can do anything. Make any order. Command any action.

"The mon is no father to the lad. He's a monster. Did ye see how thin his wee body was? He hasnae seen a decent meal in years. If ever."

Once she stopped her rant, he dropped his head into his hands. 'Twas definitely a problem, yet he wasnae sure he should take the lad from his da.

Ainslee moved close to him, standing between his spread legs. He looked up at her. "I'm reminding ye again what ye said to me numerous times. Ye are 'the laird' and all must obey ye. Ye say 'tis yer responsibility to take care of yer clan, to make sure they are well."

He sighed. "Aye."

"Then do yer duty. Tell Patrick the lad will remain here."

He felt as though his life was unraveling. He'd kenned Ainslee would be a difficult wife to manage, but after only a few weeks, she'd attempted to take control from him.

Had someone told him weeks ago that his wife would have him agreeing with her and seeing the things she suggested were truly for the best of the clan, he would have denied it. Vigorously. He was the laird. He made the decisions. The wife obeyed.

And then...

He hadn't figured on having feelings for the lass. For his heart to hurt when he saw her tears. For the warmth that flooded his insides as he watched her pick up the lad and insisted she was taking him to the castle, the fire flashing in her deep green eyes. And then demanding the wee one stay permanently.

'Twas not the way things were done. He was to marry wee, quiet, Elsbeth and continue with the way his life had been, with no concerns about bowing to his wife's wishes. In fact, not expecting to even have his wife have wishes that she expected him to bow to. Christ's toes, Elsbeth still couldna even look him in the eye while Ainslee had no trouble giving him the rough side of her tongue.

'Twas truly a mess.

* * *

HAYDON STOOD and crossed his massive arms over his chest. "When I decide if the lad should stay within the keep, I will let ye ken."

Ainslee's anger at wee Donal's da turned her against her husband. "I doona care who makes the decision. I will not allow that young lad to return to his da."

She actually backed up when Haydon moved closer. Had he always been so large? So menacing?

"Do. Not. Tell. Me. What. Ye. Will. And. Will. Not. Allow." He pointed his finger at her. "Ye ken?"

She looked away from his face. She'd never seen him so angry. Mayhaps she had gone a bit too far in making demands, but the poor lad. He was the important one in this entire conversation. If she pushed her husband too far, he might return the lad just to prove to her that he was in command, not her. But then she doubted he would do such a thing. She'd seen evidence of her husband's soft heart already.

Biting her tongue and swallowing her pride, she offered a small smile. "Aye, husband. I ken ye are the laird and make the decisions."

He regarded her with narrowed eyes, studying her for a few moments. "What game are ye playing now, lass?"

She shook her head. "No game. I want the lad to be well taken care of. 'Tis what every bairn should have." When she saw Haydon's shoulders relax, she stepped closer to him again. "'Tis sorry I am for acting the shrew and making demands, but I ne'er saw a bairn treated the way little Donal has been treated."

Haydon ran his fingers through his hair. "Aye, on that we can agree, lass." He raised his finger again and pointed at her. "But ye are not to decide what is to be done with the lad. 'Tis my decision, and I will wait upon it, and give it some thought. Ye are not the laird, and ye doona understand what the effect of a hastily made decision could be."

"Yer right, I doona understand. What damaging effect could a decision to save a wee lad have?"

"Suppose every mam and da decided their lads or lasses were giving them too much trouble? 'Twas known to happen, ye ken. Then they could appeal to me to take in their troublesome youths. We could end up running a home for wayward bairns."

Ainslee shook her head. "That is not a verra good example, husband. Taking a small, abused child away from a drunken wicked mon, who ye already were forced to toss into the dungeon once before, dosnae mean every disgruntled parent would be dropping their misbehaving youth at our doorstep."

"I grow weary of this conversation. 'Tis best if we put it aside for now."

Ainslee clamped her jaw so tight so hard she thought she would break a tooth. She had to actually bite the inside of her cheek to keep from lashing out once again. Instead, she took a deep breath, swallowed a few times and smiled. "Aye, my laird."

Her arrogant, obnoxious husband threw his head back and roared with laughter.

She turned and left the room, slamming the door so hard she thought it would fall off the hinges. The sound of his laughter echoed in her ears as she descended the stairs and turned the corner to enter the kitchen.

Arrogant oaf.

14

Within two days, Donal looked like an entirely different lad. His bruises were fading to an interesting yellow, his cuts were healing nicely, and he already looked as if he was filling out his wee body.

He no longer spent a lot of time in bed but insisted on helping in the kitchen. Ainslee believed it was because he was closer to the food. Jonet had taken a liking to the lad, and Ainslee suspected he received a lot of extras outside of the three meals served in the great hall.

Haydon hadn't yet raised the question of the lad's fate. Ainslee didn't bring it up since she still had no intention of allowing Patrick to get the lad back, and she was afraid Haydon would still demand it. Since their last argument, things had been peaceful between them.

Peaceful that was, except in bed. They seemed be of a like mind when it came to their joining. Whatever discomfort she'd had on their wedding night had disappeared. Haydon had merely to look at her in a certain way and crook his finger, and she was all over him, eager to climb into the bed and lose herself in the passion he'd found in her.

She sometimes worried that those on the same floor as their bedchamber could hear them, especially when they both grew frantic, and the headboard began to slam against the wall.

Elsbeth, of course would never comment, and generally avoided her eyes when they met each morn, but she'd caught Conall grinning at his brother more than once when they arrived to break their fast. Then her awkwardness would return.

Haydon had received several messages in the prior few days and seemed more brooding after each one. She asked him once about the missives, but he dismissed her.

He and Conall and Malcom would oftentimes retreat to Haydon's solar and stay behind closed doors for hours. A few times they sent for Darach, the soldier in charge of the men's training.

Ainslee tried her best not to worry about war arriving at their doorstep. She wasnae convinced that joining the Glencairn rebellion was a good idea. None of the clans were happy with the British invasion, but with Dornoch castle far up into the Highlands, it all seemed so far away.

She received one missive from her da which he must have sent right after arriving home from the wedding. He assured her that all was well upon his arrival. Hopefully, it would stay that way.

Ainslee walked into the kitchen to discuss the evening meal. Jonet, the absolutely wonderful cook that Haydon had found, was busy feeding extra oatcakes dripping with honey to Donal.

TO DECEIVE A HIGHLANDER

The lad smiled up at her when she entered, licking his lips of the honey that had drizzled down his chin.

"Ye like those oatcakes, do ye?" Ainslee asked.

"Aye. They're my favorite."

Jonet smiled at the lad and looked at Ainslee. "I believe the lad has a hollow leg. Elsewise, I cannot imagine where all that food goes."

He offered her a grin that melted Ainslee's heart. She placed her palm on her stomach, wondering if there were a bairn already started in her. She and Haydon had certainly been practicing enough.

"Now that the larders have been filled, perhaps we can have some roasted boar this eve, my lady?" Jonet asked.

"Aye. 'Tis a good idea. The men are about ready for something hearty."

The cook lowered her voice. "They've been practicing quite heavily in the lists too. I am hoping there isn't something coming that we all need to be concerned about." She looked at Ainslee with expectation.

There was no point in alarming the woman. "Nay. Doona fash yerself. Ye should be glad they are practicing to keep us all safe should we need it."

"Aye. And my evening prayers are that we doona need it."

From the kitchen, Ainslee sought out Elsbeth. With the chores they both had, they spent little time together until the evening meal. She was still glad to have her sister with her, however. Just knowing she was in the castle somewhere, and no' miles away helped.

One of the things da had mentioned in his missive was a reminder that while he'd allowed Elsbeth to stay, as head of the family in Dornoch, Haydon should be looking for a husband for Elsbeth.

Ainslee had brought up the subject a time or two, but her twin dinna seem interested. Sometimes Ainslee thought that Elsbeth might resent her for taking her intended husband, but when she mentioned that to her sister, she laughed, and since the wedding, she was even more grateful that Ainslee had taken her place.

For some reason that annoyed Ainslee. Haydon was difficult to get along with, aye, being arrogant, and commanding, but he was also protective, soft-hearted at times, and took care of his clan. And certainly kenned how to keep a woman pleasured in bed.

She wondered if that meant she was happy they had switched places, and not just because she had saved her sister.

There were still rooms that needed cleaning, so she headed up to the bedchamber floor to see how the servants she'd sent up there earlier were faring.

She barely made it to the room they were working in when a shout echoed throughout the keep. Unable to make out what she heard, she headed back downstairs.

Angus came flying through the back door. "Fire! The stable is on fire!"

The door to Haydon's solar flew open, and he, Conall, and Malcom stepped out.

The lad almost ran smack into Haydon. "My laird, the stable is on fire."

"Where is old Broderick?" Haydon asked as he joggled to the kitchen door, Conall and Malcom right behind him. Ainslee picked up her skirts and followed the men out the back door.

"He's out of the stable, my laird," Angus said through heavy breathing.

"The horses?"

"Most of them are out, but I think there are still one or two at the back of the building."

Haydon nodded and continued toward the burning structure.

Ainslee gasped when she stepped out the door. It appeared the entire stable was going up in flames.

* * *

HAYDON CURSED when he saw the stable. They would probably not be able to save it, but he had to make sure all the horses were out and try to at least contain the flames, so they didn't spread.

"Malcolm, start a fire line," he shouted as he picked up an axe.

Malcolm and Conall grabbed buckets and herded all the servants who had come to watch the fire into a line. They began to fill the buckets from the well and pass them along, tossing them on the growing flames.

Haydon whipped his plaid off and dunked it into the well. Wrapping it around him, he smashed the side of the stable with the axe. He backed up as the smoke came pouring out, choking him. Angus had been right, there were two horses at the back of the stable, screaming and bucking the sides of their stalls.

"Conall!" he shouted. "Drop the buckets and come here. Bring another axe with ye."

His brother joined him, and both began to break the back wall of the stable where the horses were. Within minutes there was an opening large enough for the horses to escape. They raced from the building, not stopping until Haydon could see them no more.

When they returned to the fire line, everyone from the kitchen including Ainslee, Elsbeth, and even wee Donal were frantically passing buckets. They'd gotten enough people to form two lines. The water would not save the stable, but it could prevent it from spreading.

The men came charging from the lists and formed another two lines. They worked tirelessly for a couple of hours until the entire building had collapsed and sat in a pile of wet rubble.

Soot-faced servants, soldiers, and family members sat or laid on the ground. Once he recovered, Haydon stood and walked over to old Broderick. He squatted before the mon. "What happened, do ye ken?"

The old mon looked up at him, sadness in his eyes. He'd been stablemaster since before Haydon had been born. "Nay. Wee Angus was cleaning out the stalls. I was working on some tack when I heard the lad scream, *fire*."

The mon took a deep breath. "The lad did a good job of getting the horses out." He shook his head. "'Tis sorry I am for this."

Haydon laid his hand on the man's arm. "Nay. Doona fash yerself, Broderick. These things happen. Just be grateful that ye, Angus, and the horses made it out alive. The building can be replaced."

Haydon looked around the gathering. The soldiers had started back to the lists. The kitchen help were slowly climbing to their feet. Ainslee and Elsbeth still sat on the ground with wee Donal between them.

He made his way over to Angus, seated next to his

mam. Haydon squatted again. "Tell me what happened, lad." When he noticed the lad's expression, he added, "Do no' fret. Just think carefully about what happened right before ye saw the fire and everything after that."

"Aye." Angus nodded. "I was cleaning out the front stall, ye ken, the one where Arran is kept. Old Broderick was outside, working on a bridle that had snapped. I doona remember hearing anything, but I noticed the faint smell of smoke. At first, I thought it came from the kitchen, or the bread oven which they'd been cleaning out for a few days, so I dinna pay attention to it."

While Haydon spoke with the lad, Ainslee and Elsbeth had filled buckets with water and were passing it around. They'd reached them, and handed the bucket to Angus, who took a large swallow. Haydon took it next and did the same. He handed the bucket back to Ainslee and wiped his mouth with the sleeve of his leine. "Go ahead, lad."

Angus nodded and continued. "'Twas really not the smell that got my notice, but a crackling sound. I turned and saw the south side of the stable on fire. I dinna stop to look farther but raced from the stable to the kitchen to get help.

Haydon studied the lad for a minute. Then he slapped his thighs and stood. "Ye did well, Angus. Getting help quickly might not have saved the stable, but it saved the two horses stuck in there and kept the fire from spreading."

Jonet smiled warmly at her son, and Angus ducked his head. "Thank ye, my laird."

Haydon strode toward the castle.

"Haydon, wait."

He stopped as Ainslee caught up to him. "Did you learn anything from Angus?"

"No need to be concerned, lass. I'll take care of it." He continued on.

"My laird!"

He turned, his brows raised. "Aye?"

He could see her trying to control her temper. 'Twas always fun to watch, to see if she succeeded or no'. He crossed his arms over his chest and stared at his wife. "What is it, wife?"

She raised her little chin. "I believe I have the right to ken if you learned anything from the lad."

"Is that so? And why do ye think that?"

Her temper won out, and she stomped her foot. "'Tis my home, too. I am the lady of the castle. I have every right to ken what is going on."

"No' so. Ye will ken what I wish you to ken." He waited for the explosion. 'Twas not long in coming.

His wee wife marched up to him and got close enough for him to kiss her. "The stable might have been set on fire on purpose."

"Aye."

"If so, 'twould make it a dangerous situation."

"Aye."

"If my home—our home—is in danger, it is important for me to ken that."

"Nay." He turned again and began to walk, enjoying the little distraction before he had to seriously consider what had really caused the fire at the stable. Ainslee raced ahead of him, turned and forced him to stop, lest he run over the lass. "What is it, Ainslee?"

She must have decided to switch tactics. She lowered

her voice and attempted a smile. A look that would scare small bairns. "Now, husband. Dinna ye think 'twould be good to share your concerns with yer wife?"

"Nay." When he tried to move forward this time, she put her wee hand up on his chest to stop him. 'Twas growing funnier every moment. She couldn't stop him if she hopped up into his arms.

Which was not a bad idea. Even covered in soot, her hair wild, and her sweet face flushed with anger, she tempted him. Mayhaps once he had more information on the stable event, he would order a bath in the largest bath tub the castle had and invite her to join him.

"Verra well," she said. "I understand ye do not wish to share yer life with me. That ye think a wife is no more than a womb for yer bairns, to see that yer meals are to yer liking, and everything running smoothly for the great laird. Ye want someone to bow and scrape and obey yer every command."

"Aye." He leaned forward. "Ye have finally understood the way things are supposed to work."

He laughed as he left her sputtering. It appeared the lass had a fine collection of curse words. He shook his head as he entered the keep and took a quick wash in the kitchen. The servants had returned to work, most of them having cleaned themselves up. Now 'twas time to delve into the stable fire.

* * *

Ainslee watched her husband's back as he swaggered toward the keep. After enjoying the stream of curse words that spewed from her mouth, she drew herself up and decided nay, she would not pick up the nearest rock and toss it at his self-important head. Her laird might think he kenned the way things were supposed to work, but she had no intention of becoming the wee wife who listened to his every word.

What she wanted was a bath, but with the stable fire, and the kitchen staff attempting to return to their duties, she decided helping prepare the evening meal made better use of her time.

After a quick wash, she joined the others at the worktable and began chopping vegetables. Jonet sucked in a deep breath when she saw her mistress working alongside the others. "My lady, ye should no' be chopping vegetables."

Ainslee shrugged. "No matter. The fire put us behind. With how hard all the men worked, along with everyone else, 'tis quite hungry they will all be. Ye need all the help ye can get."

Just then Elsbeth walked into the kitchen and dropped a pile of herbs in the wash bucket.

Ainslee smiled at her and nodded toward the bucket. "Ye are doing quite well with finding herbs among that mess in the garden, sister."

Elsbeth slid alongside her and picked up a knife, then began chopping. "Once I cleared away all the weeds from the months of neglect, I found a lot of herbs out there. The vegetable garden had been kept up to a certain extent, so there wasn't too much to be done there."

"Aye, the way this clan eats, 'tis a good thing we have a large vegetable garden."

Jonet turned to the sisters. "Who was in charge of the keep after Lady Sutherland died?"

"Lady Donella."

Jonet's brows rose. "The laird's sister?"

"Aye."

She turned back to cutting the meat for the stew. She shook her head. "That poor lass's head never seemed to be where the rest of her was. 'Tis a good thing the laird took a wife. 'Twas sorely needed."

It appeared everyone thought Ainslee's only position in the keep was to make sure *the laird* was happy. She glanced sideways at the cook. "Jonet, did yer husband share his troubles with ye when ye were married?"

Jonet shook her head. "Nay. I thanked the lord every day that he kept things to himself. I had enough to worry about with taking care of the house, meals, and the bairns." She waved her hand. "Let the men take care of troubles."

Well, that had gotten her nowhere. Was she so very unusual then? Were there no other women who wanted to be a partner to their husbands? To share the good and bad times? Of course, since her mam died when she and Elsbeth were too little to remember her much, and her stepmother didn't last very long after she married her da, maybe Ainslee's ideas were all wrong.

Nay.

"Ainslee, stop what yer doing lass and come to my solar." Haydon looked serious, and her stomach dropped. Was she in trouble with the mon again?

She looked over at Elsbeth. She shrugged. Ainslee couldn't help but wonder if Elsbeth was again thinking she was quite satisfied with the switch they pulled.

Haydon dinna wait for her but turned and abruptly

left the kitchen. She washed her hands and hurried after him.

Her heart began to pound when she entered the solar and saw Malcom, Conall, and Haydon sitting in a circle in the center of the room. Haydon motioned to a chair next to him and she sat. Rather than questioning him in front of his men she waited for him to speak.

"We have a problem here, lass."

God's bones. What had she done this time?

She licked her dry lips. "What is that, my laird?"

"We have reason to believe the stable fire was set."

Ainslee looked around at the dark expressions on the men's faces. Surely, they dinna think she had something to do with it? "I doona understand. Although I suggested it, why would someone set the stable on fire?"

"As a distraction." Haydon leaned back and crossed his arms over his chest. "Do ye remember I told ye some time back that William Cunningham had learned there was a spy among the clans planning the uprising?"

"Aye."

"As ye are probably aware, I have been receiving missives about the plans recently."

She nodded.

"Before the fire started, we," he waved at the other two men, "were discussing them. When the fire broke out, we all rushed to the stable to help."

"Aye?"

"While we were all battling the fire, someone came into the solar and removed all the missives."

Her jaw dropped in surprise. "Then that means—"

"Aye. The spy working for the British is here in Dornoch."

15

Things at Castle Dornoch had been in a frenzy for two weeks. Once Haydon had determined the spy was among his people, he sent a missive to William Cunningham and suggested they call a gathering at Dornoch Castle of the clans committed to the rebellion to discuss the matter.

As far as he was concerned, this was the best place to meet. It would be an easy matter to pass along to whoever was snooping for the enemy whatever information they wanted the British to learn. False dates, false movements, false plans.

Ainslee entered Haydon's solar where he was going over numbers for the final planting to be done for the season. "Haydon, I tried my best to get all the chambers finished before yer guests arrive. There were so many in need of refreshing that we dinna get them all."

He dropped his writing instrument and leaned back in his chair. "Aye."

"Do ye ken yet how many chambers we will need?

Also, how many guests. I assume some will bring their wives—"

"Nay. 'Tis a gathering of chieftains and lairds. Women have no place in that."

He smothered his laugh as the muscle in her right eye began to twitch.

She took a deep breath. "Since there is much to do before the arrival of the men, I will no' waste my time sewing up stitches on yer hard head from the bowl I'd like to throw at ye."

"I appreciate that, wife."

"However, since I am a laird's wife, and *I will be here* taking care of things, making sure everyone has enough to eat and a warm comfortable place to sleep, I need numbers. Haven't ye said many times a woman's place is to see to the running of the castle?"

"Aye."

He almost regretted her not firing back at him at his goading remark about the wives. God's bones he enjoyed sparring with her. However, since their heated disagreements generally ended up with him scooping her up into his arms and hustling up to their bedchamber, 'twas probably for the best since they did have a lot to do before the clan leaders arrived on the morrow.

"Then how many should I prepare for?"

He thought for a moment. "We're expecting four heads of clans along with William. They will all be bringing aides and escorts with them, possibly as many as twenty to fifty each."

"A lot of food."

"Aye. But the larders should be full since the men have been hunting daily for a couple of weeks now."

"And when are they expected?"

"When I count the time it took for William to get back to me on the information I sent him after the stable fire, and how long it would take for him to send out his own missives and then the others to make things right and leave their homes, I think ye should plan for just about any time now."

HAYDON'S PREDICTION had been correct, and the first of the chieftains appeared that afternoon. Sir Magnus MacDuff was the first to arrive, along with his two top advisors, Nelson Sommers, and Graham McDougal, along with thirty warriors.

The stream of guests continued for the rest of that day and all the next. By the evening meal on the second day, all the expected men had arrived. Haydon was proud of his wife, and how she handled everything, but having done the same for her da's castle, she was well trained.

He'd tried to compliment her on her work, but she glared at him and sashayed away.

'Twas time for the first evening meal since the men had arrived, and as if thinking about her made her appear, Haydon looked up from the dais in the great hall as his wife entered the room. She was a vision, in a blue and gold gown with a small, gold leaf wreath circling her lush, dark red hair. It annoyed him to see all the male appreciation sent in her direction.

Before she could cross the room, he hopped up and joined her, taking her arm in his. "You look lovely this evening, my lady."

Apparently, complimenting her on her appearance

worked better than doing so on her work. She smiled warmly, and he had the urge to toss her over his shoulder and skip the evening meal. "Thank you, my laird."

"Sutherland, introduce yer wife. Most of us haven't met her." Sir Thomas shouted from his seat at the dais.

"Aye. And a bonnie lass she is," MacDuff added as he stood and bowed to her. A handsome mon, he was charming and from what Haydon had heard, had no problem finding lasses to warm his bed, despite having a wife for several years.

Haydon pondered on how he could rearrange that handsome face with his fists. But playing the host, he said, "May I present Lady Sutherland." He went down the row of men, naming each one. "Sir Magnus MacDuff, John Middleton, Sir Ewan Cameron, Robert Lilburne, George Monck, and Sir Thomas Morgan."

Just then Elsbeth joined them, and the men looked back and forth between the two lasses. "Ye lucky devil, Sutherland. Two bonnie lasses," Sir Ewan said.

"Aye, this is Lady Elsbeth. No need for me to tell ye she and my wife are twins."

His sister-in-law gave a graceful dip, but then hurried to Ainslee's side. Haydon looked the men over again, considering the task his father-in-law had charged him with. To find a husband for Elsbeth. He easily dismissed them all.

Servants entered the room, carrying trenchers for each mon and the lasses. Then platters of roasted boar, pigeon, venison, rabbit, various fishes, and large bowls of vegetables were placed along the table.

"Sutherland, I hope yer not planning on keeping those

bonnie lasses to yerself all night." Once again MacDuff ogled Elsbeth and Ainslee.

"These bonnie lasses are my wife and sister by marriage. They are under my protection, and I warn ye and anyone else that they are not to be touched." He wanted to add, 'or looked at' but that would have been a bit too much. He did thank the good lord that Donella was too shy to sit at the table, or it would be three lasses he had to be concerned about.

Graham threw back his head and laughed. "Sounds to me as though yer wife has a firm rope around yer neck, Sutherland."

Ainslee leaned close to him. "Ignore them, husband. They are stupid men if they believe I would look twice at any of them. Nor Elsbeth."

Haydon had no reason to disbelieve her, but he was still not comfortable with all the attention the lasses were getting. Maybe he would insist Ainslee remain in their bedchamber for the extent of their visit. Then he almost laughed, thinking about what sort of an explosion that would cause.

Luckily—for the men, anyway—talk soon turned to the travel from their homes to Dornoch, and the lands they had to trek across to do that. Obviously, nothing of note would be discussed outside of the meeting room since they had no idea who the spy was.

Tomorrow, they would begin their strategy meetings and decide what false information they wanted to leak among the staff. It bothered him that one of his people was a traitor.

He groaned as the last of the food had been returned to the kitchen and one of the younger aides with Sir

Thomas requested music. The only lasses available for dancing were Elsbeth and Ainslee. Not having a female partner had never stopped a determined Highlander before, since they were known to dance by themselves, but he was still annoyed at the looks his wife was receiving.

Three of the servants were accomplished with the fiddle and flute, so within a few minutes, tables had been pushed aside and the music began.

Haydon leaned near Ainslee's ear. "I believe 'twoud be good if ye and yer sister retired for the night."

* * *

AINSLEE DIDN'T KEN whether she should stab his hand with her eating knife or laugh herself silly. In some ways, she was pleased that he was acting so protective of her, but in another way she felt insulted. Did he trust her so little, then? Did he believe she would accept an invitation into one of these men's bed just because they glanced in her direction?

"My Lady, may I request a dance?" Robert Lilbourne stood before her with his hand out.

"Her feet hurt," Haydon said, tapping his finger on the table.

She looked at him, her mouth agape. "They do no'."

"Her ankle, then. She twisted her ankle earlier today. The poor lass can hardly walk."

Ainslee just shook her head and stood. "I will be happy to dance with ye, Robert." She cast Haydon an exasperated glance and joined Robert in the dance area.

"Yer husband seems quite fond of ye, my lady." Robert glanced between her and a glaring Haydon.

"Hmm. Yes, that he is."

There was no more time, or breath, for further conversation because the lively tune the fiddler played kept them hopping and dancing. As she turned, she saw Conall and Elsbeth dancing. Ainslee was grateful for that, since she kenned Elsbeth would not be comfortable if one of the men were to ask her to dance.

In fact, it appeared Conall was steering Elsbeth further from the dancing, and closer to the stairs. With a quick turn of his arm, he released her, and she hurried away, never turning back.

For the next hour or so, Ainslee was passed along from one mon to the next. Perhaps her feet hadn't hurt before, but they did now. She looked over at Haydon who had been sitting, with his arms crossed over his chest, scowling at her since the music had begun.

Perhaps it was time to settle her husband. When the music stopped this time, she held up her palm as another mon approached her. "I think I've had enough for tonight, Sir Ewan." Before he could protest, she made her way over to Haydon and collapsed on the bench alongside him.

"Have ye had yer fill of dancing, lass?"

"Aye."

"Good." He stood and took her hand. After nodding to the men left in the great hall, he put his arm around her waist and hustled her from the room, up the stairs, and into the bedchamber.

The rest of the night was a blur.

. . .

Two days later, Ainslee reached over to find Haydon's large part of the bed empty and cold. Again. It dinna appear to be too late in the morn, however, since the sun was barely up. She had a lot to do with the keep full, so she quickly washed and dressed and hurried downstairs to the kitchen, braiding her hair as she went.

Jonet was busy cooking a large cauldron of porridge, sweat running down her face. The lasses at the table were chopping an ever-growing pile of vegetables. Elsbeth had apparently been assigned slicing all the loaves of bread, fresh from the oven. The baking oven had been left outside, and Haydon had the men build a structure around it to protect it from the weather but keep it away from the kitchen.

"What can I do to help?" Ainslee asked.

Jonet turned to her. "Oh, my lady, ye have guests. I told ye yesterday, ye shouldn't be here in the kitchen with us. 'Tis not proper."

"No worries, Jonet. I have been known to be improper at times." She winked at the woman.

Elsbeth snorted.

Given Haydon's actions with the men's attention to her, she'd decided it was probably best for her to spend as little time as possible with them. He'd been so sweet when they were alone that she forgave him for his poor manners the first eve the men had arrived.

What did his behavior mean? Did he so care for her that he was afraid to lose her? Or was it simply a matter of pride and possession? Most likely the last. Haydon had stated since the beginning that he wanted a wife for breeding and running his keep. Nothing more was added. Such as caring or even love.

What frightened her was the fact that she was afraid she was falling in love with the arrogant oaf. That was never her intention. 'Twas to help her sister out. It had never occurred to her that she might grow to truly care for the mon.

Nay.

Conall entered the kitchen, glancing around the room, then moved next to Ainslee who as yet hadn't found a job to do. "Ainslee, Haydon requests that ye join them to break yer fast."

That was a surprise, given his possessive behavior, but she followed Conall down to the great hall.

The men appeared to be in a rowdy argument. Flushed faces and waving of arms continued as voices raised higher and higher. However, once William spotted her walking toward the table, he shushed the group, and they all fell silent.

Was this the reason Haydon had wanted her to join them? To settle the men down with the presence of a lady?

He stood. "Good morn, wife."

"My laird." She gave a slight dip.

Several hearty and not so hearty welcomes and 'good days' followed her as she made her way to her husband's side.

Before she had a chance to take one sip of ale, the servants began to carry in huge bowls of porridge, platters of bread and cheese, and oatcakes. The men made quick work of the food, but Ainslee found her appetite a bit short and decided to just sip her ale.

Haydon turned to her. "We will be meeting for most of the morning, then the soldiers asked for a competition.

Since the weather appears to be pleasant, we decided to hold it in the lists this afternoon."

How surprisingly nice of her husband to tell her this. Mayhaps things were improving between them.

"The reason I'm telling ye this is because we will want a bit of a celebration this eve. Most of the men will be leaving on the morrow, so 'tis a good way to end the meetings."

"Already? They've only been here two days."

"Aye. But remember the reason for the meeting was to pass along false information. We also finished up some of the details about the uprising. Most are anxious to return to their homes and continue to prepare for war."

Hearing that word made her shudder. Why couldn't men just get along, why did they always have to be taking up swords and charging at each other? 'Twas something she would never understand.

"Verra well, I will ask Jonet to prepare a special meal."

He reached for her hand and kissed her knuckles. "How are ye this morn, lass?"

Kenning exactly what he meant since they'd been a bit more enthusiastic than usual the night before, she felt a slight blush rise to her cheeks. She raised her chin. "I am well, my laird. And ye? Have I worn ye out?"

He burst out laughing, drawing the attention of some of the men. "I doubt it, lass."

"God's bones, Sutherland, cannae ye wait until tonight to romance yer lass? Yer making us all jealous with yer bonnie wife." MacDuff smiled, but there was something behind that smile that troubled her. She'd seen him following her with his eyes every time they'd been in the same room. Mayhaps it was a good thing that the gathering would be ending with them leaving on the morrow.

She excused herself and headed to the kitchen to alert Jonet that the evening meal would need to be a feast. 'Twould be best if she gathered a few of the other servants and put them all to work in the kitchen. Of one thing she was certain. She wanted to watch the competition on the lists. Although 'twas a competition between the warriors, she had a feeling that Haydon would be challenged, and she wanted to see her warrior in action.

The thought brought tingles to her insides.

The kitchen staff and those who had been pulled from other duties were all busy when Elsbeth and Ainslee left to see the men compete. For as little bit of an appetite as she'd had that morn, she was ravenous now and had a few slices of bread, cold meat, and cheese before they left the kitchen.

They dinna need directions as to where the men were. The shouting, bragging, and general boasting going on was almost comical.

From what they could see, the clan chiefs had each picked their top warrior to fight. The winner of the first round would fight the warrior of the next group, and so on down until the one left standing was declared the winner.

Haydon and Conall leaned against the outer wall, their arms crossed, watching the men. Malcom spoke to his men, and eventually settled on a warrior who looked as though he'd survived many battles. The younger lads were anxious to compete, but dinna have the experience to go up against another clan's top mon.

Once the competition began, 'twas obvious the men

enjoyed the challenges. The whooping and hollering were earsplitting. One by one, the men were eliminated until just MacDuff's mon and Haydon's mon were left. The castle staff had left their chores and streamed out when they'd heard their top mon was to compete in the final round.

David Sutherland faced off with his opponent. The men circled each other, knees bent, their swords snug in their hands. The cheering began as the warriors clashed, retreated, and clashed again. 'Twas obvious they were well matched, but after about five minutes, David spun, and taking MacDuff's mon by surprise, brought his sword up under the other mon's and whipped the blade from his hand. The warrior stumbled, then fell to the ground. David placed the tip of his sword at the man's throat, his boot on his chest.

The cheering from the castle staff and soldiers must have been heard across the border. David grinned, moved his sword away from the mon's neck, and reached out to help the warrior up.

MacDuff glared at his mon and then at Haydon. He stomped up to him, poking him in the chest. "Yer mon cheated."

Haydon straightened, as did Conall. "The mon did not cheat. He was clever. Took your mon by surprise."

"I doona agree with the outcome." He stepped back and said, "I challenge ye. Let's see how the great Sutherland, Laird of Dornoch competes. Or has it been too long since ye held a sword? Have yer men been fighting for ye?"

Ainslee gripped Elsbeth's hand. "Nay. I doona like this. MacDuff is evil, I can see it in his eyes."

Elsbeth shook her head. "Nay, sister. Ye doona have enough faith in yer husband."

She licked her dry lips as Haydon slid his sword from its scabbard, removed his plaid and leine, and smiled at the mon. "Yer challenge is accepted, MacDuff."

16

Haydon had been looking for an excuse to pummel MacDuff since the mon had first arrived and made eyes at Ainslee. He saw the way the mon looked at her when he thought Haydon didn't see. The lecher had been wrong. Haydon had been watching his every move.

He was grateful for MacDuff's challenge and was ready for it. After stripping, he strode toward the area where the challenges had taken place. MacDuff had stripped down also and grinned at the young lasses who ogled his chest.

Good, let the mon become confident. That made it easier to beat him.

The crowd grew silent as knees bent, they circled each other.

MacDuff grinned. "That's a fine lass ye have there, Sutherland. It must feel good to slide yer staff between her soft thighs every night."

Haydon tightened his grip on the sword, but his concentration had been broken.

"Aye, mon. I wouldn't mind taking yer place one night," MacDuff continued, "just let me ken when ye can't handle the challenge. I'm certain I can pleasure the lass better than ye."

Haydon swung his sword, and MacDuff stepped back, laughing.

"Do ye enjoy running yer hands up and down her curves? I've thought about doing it."

Haydon growled and moved in, swinging. MacDuff stepped back, the grin gone from his face. "What's wrong, Sutherland, not sure if yer lass wouldn't enjoy another mon between her legs?"

MacDuff made sure his comments could not be heard by anyone except Haydon and were obviously muttered to distract him. Unfortunately, he was doing a good job. Haydon took a deep breath and let his years of training and fighting take over. No matter what MacDuff said, he would focus on beating the bastard into the dust.

MacDuff must have noticed the switch in Haydon's focus. No longer did he throw out disgusting words, and his smirk disappeared.

Haydon had taken back control.

The fight went on, the sound of swords clashing ringing against the castle walls. They parried back and forth, both well-trained warriors at their best. MacDuff took a stab to his shoulder and Haydon gritted his teeth when MacDuff swiped below his waist and slashed his thigh. The pain was incredible, but he would not let his men down.

He kenned with the blood he was losing he'd begin to

weaken soon, so he had to make one final attempt to fell MacDuff. With one solid swipe at MacDuff's sword, the weapon flew from his hands and the momentum caused the mon to fall back, landing on his arse. Within seconds Haydon was standing above him, his boot on the mon's chest, breathing hard, blood dripping from his wound. He placed his sword at the challenger's neck. "I should kill ye for what ye said about my wife."

MacDuff just stared at him. "'Twas only a ploy."

"Aye. A dangerous one. I want ye out of my castle within the next two hours." He stepped back and raised his fist in the air to the cheers of the crowd. He reached down and pulled MacDuff up, then turned his back and walked away.

Ainslee raced up to him. "Haydon, ye are cut."

"Quiet lass, 'tis nothing." Despite the excruciating pain, he walked to the keep without limping, accepting congratulations and slaps on the back. The pain was so bad he thought he would either swoon like a lass or bring up his last meal.

His wife said nothing further, but followed him into the keep, up the stairs, and to their bedchamber. Once inside with the door closed, she turned on him. "Haydon, that is a serious cut. Yer losing blood. Lie down on the bed. I will need to sew ye up."

Finally, he gave up and collapsed on the bed, holding his leg. "It hurts like the devil, lass," he said.

She shook her head. "Lie back, and I will get some supplies."

He leaned up on his elbows. "Doona speak of the injury outside this room."

She placed her hands on her hips. "Everyone saw ye get cut."

"It doona matter. All ye need to say is it was a scratch." He laid back and grimaced. "Bring whisky, too."

* * *

AINSLEE HAD NEARLY COLLAPSED at the sight of Haydon's thigh being sliced by MacDuff's sword. She kenned right away it was a serious cut and verra painful. But being Haydon, he acted as though 'twas nothing.

How he finished the match and even won was a true statement of the mon's determination and strength. She tried not to be proud of him because she'd been sure the arrogant oaf was going to bleed to death before the match ended.

She gathered the herbs she needed from the kitchen just as the rest of the staff was returning from the lists, chattering gaily, commenting on the power of their laird.

"How is his lairdship? That seemed to be a serious cut he took there," Jonet asked as she tied her apron around her middle.

"Nay," she lied. "'Twas not serious. I just need to patch him up a bit." God's bones that lie came out so easily.

She filled a bucket with warm water, snatched some clean linen pieces, a jug of whisky, and headed back upstairs.

Haydon looked as though he'd passed out, but when she closed the door, he opened his eyes. "Thank ye, lass."

Ainslee got busy cleaning the wound, pouring whisky on it—which brought Haydon right up into her face with a howl—then sewed the cut closed. With shaking hands, he reached for the cup of whisky and downed what was left.

"This is a deep cut, Haydon," she said as she smoothed honey over the stitches. "Ye should stay off yer feet for a few days."

He grimaced as he shifted his body. "Nay. I must be at the feast tonight."

She wagged her finger at him. "But ye will stay in bed for the rest of the day before the evening meal."

Sweat broke out on his forehead when he attempted to stand. He blew out a breath and sat back down. "I cannae hide in my room like a sulking bairn."

"I will make a deal with ye."

He glanced at her sideways, his eyes narrowed. "What deal?"

"I will pass the word that yer gone until the evening meal because yer dealing with a clan member's emergency." She raised her hand when he opened his mouth to speak. "I will mix up a potion to help ye sleep for only a couple hours."

The mon must have been in a great deal of pain because he agreed. Before he could change his mind, she mixed up the sleep potion with the little bit of water left in the bucket. "Here, drink this."

Once he took the last swallow, he looked at her with a slight smile and put his hand out. "I ken I would sleep much better if ye were beside me."

She couldn't help but smile. "Nay. I appreciate the invitation, but I need to account for yer absence and make sure everything is ready for the feast."

"MacDuff and his group are leaving before the festivities."

"Because he lost?"

"Nay, because I told him to leave." When she raised her brows, he said, "Doona fash yerself over it."

Whatever the reason, she would be glad to see the mon depart. She didn't care for the way he watched her, or the way he challenged Haydon because he said David had cheated. He was not an honorable mon.

The afternoon passed quickly as she busied herself with chores for the special supper. She used flowers and herbs to make the great hall smell good and look decorative. The meal was going well in the kitchen, and the time had arrived for her to check Haydon's wound and help him downstairs. As she passed through the great hall on her way to her bedchamber, she was stopped when a hand reached out from the shadows and grabbed her wrist. "Wait a minute, lass."

Her temper rose when she looked into MacDuff's eyes. His bloodshot eyes, which told her he'd been drinking. She thought Haydon said he and his men were leaving right away.

"Ye think yer mon is so verra braw, aye?"

She tugged her arm, but he held fast. "I suggest ye do as my husband asked and leave the castle."

He waved his hand. "My men are preparing everything. I just want to invite ye to come with us."

Her eyes grew so wide she thought they would pop out of her head. "Go with ye? Have ye lost yer mind, MacDuff? I have no intention of going with ye or anyone else. No' that it's any of yer business, but I am quite content with my husband. Who, I might add, is an honorable mon."

Catching her completely unaware, he tugged her

closer. "I like a lass with spirit. We could do well together." Then the horrid mon covered her face with his hands and placed his mouth on hers.

At first, she was so stunned she did nothing. Then all her senses kicked in. Including her temper. Instead of fighting the mon, she merely raised her knee and with all her might, slammed it into his private parts.

He was writhing, wailing, and rolling on the floor as she walked away.

AINSLEE SLOWLY AWOKE, unable to move her neck without pain. Once again, she'd spent the night in the chair next to Haydon as he fought the fever that had kept him almost delirious for three days.

Fortunately, the fever hadn't arrived until after all the guests had left, so Hadyon was able to play the stalwart warrior and not reveal how much pain he was in from the wound.

Rotating her neck, she felt a little bit better. She leaned over and felt Haydon's head. Cool to the touch. The fever had broken. It had done the same thing a few times in the past few days but came back again. Hopefully not this time.

He opened his eyes. "Ainslee."

Tears flooded her eyes. She told herself it was because she hadn't gotten a good night's sleep in days, but the voice inside told her she was glad to hear the arrogant oaf speak.

Her voice shook. "Are ye feeling better?"

He smiled, the first one she'd seen in a while. "Aye, but verra thirsty."

She hopped up and filled a cup with ale. "Doona drink it too fast."

Once he finished, he handed the goblet to her. "How long have I been out?"

"This is the third day of yer fever." She smoothed the hair back from his forehead. "I was worried we would lose ye."

"Nay. I'm too stubborn to die." He shifted a bit and grimaced. "How is the wound doing?"

"Ye mean the slight scratch ye got in the swordfight with MacDuff?" She smirked and stood. "Let's take a look."

She sat alongside him and pulled the sheet down. Moving the bandage aside she studied the wound. "Actually, healing nicely. No pus or nasty fluid."

"And I ken that I have ye to thank for that."

She shrugged. "'Tis my job."

He reached up and covered her cheek with his large hand. "Nay, lass. Ye put a lot of caring into what ye do."

The tears that had been gathering in her eyes slowly slid down her cheeks. She laid her head on his chest and closed her eyes. He would not die. She would be married to the arrogant oaf for many years.

Thank you, God.

Sitting up, she wiped the tears from her cheeks. "I will ask Jonet for some broth for ye, then clean yer bandage again."

He grimaced. "What I need more than that lass, is a chamber pot."

The blood rushed to her face, and she stood up. "Of course. I will fetch one for ye and leave ye to yer business while I get water and clean cloths and some broth." Before she left the room, she said, "Will ye need assistance?"

"Nay. I will do just fine."

Grateful for that, she left the bedchamber and headed to the kitchen. "Jonet, the laird is awake!"

The cook threw her head back. "Praise the Lord!"

"Wonderful news," Elsbeth said as she looked up from where she was working on cleaning and drying herbs.

"I'll need some broth. Do ye have any on hand?"

"Aye. I made a batch just waiting for my laird to awaken and send it up to him. It has lots of meat bones in it, so it will help him heal."

Donal raced into the kitchen and came to an abrupt stop when he saw Ainslee. "Is my laird feeling better?"

She hadn't seen the lad in a while since she'd been busy with their visitors, and then with tending to Haydon. Donal looked like any other lad, bright eyes, a full, healthy body, and shining hair. Which was falling over his forehead, reminding her he needed a haircut.

"Aye, Donal, he is feeling better. His fever broke, and now he is getting some broth. Would ye like to come upstairs with me and see him for a minute?"

The lad jumped up and down. "Aye. I would like that." He raced ahead of her and was already in the bedchamber, sitting next to Haydon on the bed when Ainslee arrived.

"Be careful, Donal. Ye don't want to bump the laird's wound."

Haydon smiled. "'Tis fine, wife. I hope ye brought me more than that cup of broth."

"Broth is good for you. You're recovering, and the meat bones used to make the broth will help ye heal."

"Wife, no mon was ever healed by drinking broth. I prefer the meat that was used to make the broth."

She shook her head. "Ye might be ready, but yer stomach has been empty for three days."

"My stomach was empty for three days a lot of time," Donal said in a verra cheerful tone.

That brought the conversation to a halt. Ainslee looked at Haydon and shook her head.

Fortunately, it appeared that Patrick might have forgotten his son, since they hadn't seen the mon since they took Donal from him.

"Well, yer stomach won't be empty anymore."

The lad entertained them with stories of his adventures while Haydon was suffering the fever. After a while, it appeared Haydon was growing tired, so Ainslee shuffled Donal from the room.

"Lass, I'm serious. I need some food. Doona tell me how good the broth is for me. I. Need. Food."

"Very well. I'll see what Jonet has that might not hurt yer stomach too much. Maybe some porridge?"

He glared at her. "Wife. If ye bring anything up here except a decent stew with a lot of warm bread, I'll toss ye over my lap and give ye a fine whipping."

She laughed as she backed up. "Ah, but ye need to catch me first." She hurried from the room, feeling much better since her husband was threatening her.

Things were back to normal.

17

*A*inslee and Haydon fought for days over him staying in bed. Finally, three days after his fever broke, she entered the bedchamber to see her husband sitting on the bed, bent over, attempting to pull on his boots.

"What are ye doin' ye fool mon? Do ye want to rip out those stitches?"

He huffed in frustration. "I am leaving the bed. I have work to do, and nothing is being done while I lie here like a sick old mon."

"Ye are going nowhere until I check that wound."

"Just because I've been sick, doona think ye can tell me what to do, wife. I am yer laird. I tell *ye* what to do."

Ainslee crossed her arms over her chest and tapped her foot. "Ach, ye impossible arrogant oaf. Go ahead, then, tear open the stitches, but doona think I will sew ye back up again."

Haydon's shoulders slumped as if all the air had left

him. "I promise I will not do too much, but I must tend to some things."

Conceding so fast told her how very weary her husband was. 'Twas no surprise since the cut he received had done a lot of damage. In fact, he was lucky he had not lost the leg.

"One thing we must do right away is plant the bait for our traitor," he said, having seemed to have forgotten about his struggle with his boots.

"Aye, I agree with ye. Do ye have in mind what we should do?"

Haydon rubbed his chin. "I do. I'm going to have to depend on ye, lass. When I go downstairs—"

"—yer no' going downstairs—"

"—when I go downstairs, I will place the writings we decided on at our meeting in the top drawer of the desk in my solar. Ye will speak with the staff and make it known that no one is to clean my solar for a few days since there are important papers there that cannot be moved."

"Aye. 'Tis a good idea."

He nodded. "I will try to have Conall or Malcom keep an eye on the solar. The only person who should try to enter it will be whoever is looking for information to pass along to the British."

"Will ye stop him, then?"

"Nay. The idea is for him to pass along the wrong report. But we still want to ken who it is to place him under guard once he's done the deed."

After hesitating, apparently caught up in his thoughts, he said, "I will give ye one more day for me to stay in this room. However, I will not lie about in this bloody bed. If ye will gather ledgers I need to work on, and the papers I refer to and bring them up to me, I can do some work up here."

Having won that battle, Ainslee left Haydon with the breakfast tray she had brought to him to gather the things he requested.

Perhaps his yielding so quickly was a sign that he was prepared to see her as a partner, not just as a way to produce bairns or act as chatelaine for the castle.

After locating the notes for the spy and the ledger that Haydon intended to work on, Ainslee once again returned to their bedchamber. The mon had managed to make it over to the comfortable chair in front of the fire. Catching her frown, he said. "'Twas not too bad walking, actually. I think it might do me well to walk a bit."

Once he went through the papers, he held them out to her. "These are the ones. Place them in the center drawer and then begin telling all the servants and maids, even the kitchen help, that they are not to clean the room until told to do so."

She nodded and left him already crouched over his ledger. Before she could close the door, however, he said, "Send Rodric up to me. I have some questions about this last yield."

Again, she was off running errands. She found the steward in his own little room on the other side of the keep. Once she'd dispatched him to her husband, she began her campaign of placing the papers in the desk in the solar and then telling the staff they were not to clean the room.

Since Haydon had agreed to remain in their bedchamber for one more day, she decided to have Cook prepare a special meal for just the two of them, which she would eat with him.

Things were running smoothly, and she believed this could be a very pleasant life for her. Elsbeth was settled, and while Ainslee wouldn't say her sister was happy, she was at least content. As well as happy to be avoiding marriage to a mon Da would pick for her.

Over the last few weeks, Ainslee thought more and more that she might be carrying Haydon's bairn. She suffered a sour stomach in the mornings, then a ravenous appetite at the nooning, and inevitably followed that up with a short nap. Lately, that had been in their bed while curled up alongside her husband as he rested.

She hadn't said anything to Haydon yet since she wanted to be sure. The lack of her courses was another sign, but she hadn't been married verra long and 'twas quite possible her body was merely making adjustments.

But deep in her heart she knew a bairn grew inside her.

"My lady, I have yer meal all ready for ye and my laird." Jonet greeted her as she entered the kitchen to advise the staff she'd missed before about the papers in Haydon's solar.

"Thank ye, Jonet. I hope I dinna put ye through too much extra work."

"There is no extra work for my laird. I'm still grateful for this job as well as my lad's in the stable. 'Tis the difference between seeing my bairns well fed or watching them starve."

Ainslee patted the woman's arm. "That will ne'er happen. I'm sure my laird has told ye to ne'er put yerself in that position again. He is yer protector. Any trouble ye have becomes his trouble."

"He is the best of men, my lady. Ye are truly blessed to be married to him." Jonet waved at one of the lads bringing the bread from the baking oven outside the kitchen. "Here, Iain, carry this tray upstairs for yer lady."

"Before we leave, I would have all of yer attention," Ainslee said. "There are very important papers in my laird's solar. 'Tis vital that no one enter the room to clean until the missives have been sent off."

"Aye, my lady," could be heard from various workers.

Satisfied that she had spread the word as best she could, she smiled at the lad carrying the tray. "Thank ye, Iain, for yer help."

As she and Iain entered her bedchamber, Haydon surprised her by not appearing at all worn out from an afternoon of work, but then he was a strong mon.

"Our evening meal has arrived," she said. She placed a jug of wine she'd taken from the buttery and placed it on the table where the lad had set the tray of food.

Haydon looked at the tray with eager eyes. Fragrant roasted venison, fish, vegetables, chunks of cheese, and warm bread and butter wafted throughout the room. "Aye, 'tis a fine feast."

"Thank ye, lad," Ainslee said as she removed the food from the tray and placed it on the small table between the two chairs in front of the fire.

"Is this a celebration?" Haydon asked.

She could tell by the look on his face that he suspected what she'd been trying to hide for a few weeks. Mayhaps this was a good time to share her secret. She poured them both a cup of wine and handed one to him.

His brows rose. "What is the occasion, wife?"

Her eyes filled with tears, and her voice shook. "I believe we have a bairn on the way, my laird."

The look on her husband's face was one she would ne'er forget. Pride, fear, happiness, and possibly even love shone from his eyes. He raised his cup of wine. "'Tis a happy day, my lady. A happy day, indeed."

Being ravenously hungry once again, Ainslee dug into her food. Between the two of them, they finished all that cook had sent up. Haydon patted his stomach and leaned back. "I need to hold court soon."

"Aye?"

"I usually run court twice a moon, but with our guests and this bothersome scratch on my leg, 'tis past time. I dinna want to hobble into the great hall in front of my people, so I'm planning one for another week. My wound should be better by then."

"I remember my da running court. He allowed Elsbeth and me to sit alongside him once we were no longer young lasses to offer our opinion and advice."

Haydon's brows shot up to his hairline. "Sit with him?"

She frowned. "Aye. Of course, when my step-mother was alive, she accompanied him, but when she passed away, he allowed us to participate with him. 'Twas a partnership he said."

Haydon huffed. "No partnership in this clan, wife. I sit in judgement of the court, and no one gives advice."

Her eyes narrowed. "Are ye telling me I will have no place as head of this clan?"

"That is what I am telling ye. I am the laird. I run the court, just as I am charged with the care and control of the clan. I doona need anyone to 'advise' me."

Ainslee just about lost her breath.

"I dinna believe it! Ye were serious when ye said over and over that as yer wife, I am restricted to producing heirs and running the keep. I have no other place in the castle or in yer life."

"Nay, lass. 'Tis not true. Ye are verra important in my life."

She huffed. "As long as I stay in my place."

"Aye."

Ainslee stood, gathered up the remains from their meal, and stomped from the room. She would have loved to slam the door shut, but with the tray in her hands she couldna.

* * *

HAYDON WATCHED in both shock and amusement as his wife stomped from the room. Partners! He was laird. He held court. He made the decisions. His da never had mam alongside him when he did. He shook his head. Her da certainly put crazy ideas in his daughters' heads.

When it grew late and Ainslee had not returned, Haydon hobbled down the corridor, tapping on doors of empty bedchambers. Finally, a soft, "Aye" answered his knock.

He entered to see his wife all comfortable and cozy in the bed. She wore her usual night dress that he generally had off her within seconds of entering their bed. Her hair was brushed and braided, and she was working on some embroidery or such and looked up at him with a puzzled expression. "Did you want something, my laird?"

It appeared she was more disgruntled than he'd realized. "Aye. I want ye in my bed where ye've been since we married."

She shook her head and looked back down at the work in her hands.

He came closer to the bed. "Ainslee, I doona ken what yer trying to do, but ye are to return to our bed."

"I'm sorry, my laird, but since I revealed to ye just hours ago that I am carrying yer bairn, one of my duties as a wife is finished for another seven or eight months. I shall be sleeping in here until 'tis time to start on another bairn."

He was left speechless. For about a minute. He gritted his teeth. "Ye will return to our bed."

She carefully placed her work on her lap and looked up at him. "I will no'. Ye laid out my duties quite clearly since the day I arrived at Dornoch. I feel I am doing a good job of acting as the castle chatelaine, and it appears my other duty has been fulfilled." She patted her still flat stomach.

'Twas impossible with his injury to scoop her up and carry her back to his bed. *Their* bed. His wife was stubborn enough to continue this until the bairn was born.

He drew himself up. "I am yer laird. I order ye to return to our bed."

"Nay."

He hobbled closer until he was towering over her. Grown warriors had turned a sickly pale when they'd come into this close contact with him. His wife ignored him. "Ainslee."

"Aye." She continued to work. He reached down grabbed the cloth from her hands and tossed it over his shoulder. "Ye will look at me when I speak."

She sighed as if he were a mere annoyance. She raised her head, and he swore he saw mirth in her eyes. Mixed with anger.

"Think ye I will change my mind about the court if ye do this?" he asked.

Anger overtook the mirth, and she sat up straight and stared him in the eye. "'Tis not just court, my laird. If I canna be a full partner to ye, and the two of us work as a team, then I will perform only what duties you've ordered me to do. If ye canna see the advantage of having a wife who ye can confide in, and seek advice from on occasion, then ye are more stubborn, hard-headed, and arrogant than even I thought."

With that tirade, she blew out the candle alongside her, turned her back on him and snuggled down in the bedcovers. "I bid ye good night, my laird."

Aside from striking her, which he would never, ever do, he turned and hobbled back to his bedchamber. The stream of curses coming from his mouth would alarm the devil himself.

Grumbling as he removed his clothes, he climbed into bed and laid on his back, his hands behind his head. Da never had anyone else with him when he ran the court. And his mam was happy to leave all the troublesome matters to him. Ne'er did she want to ken what Da discussed with his aides, or why he decided what he did when he held court. Bloody hell, she never even attended court.

Partners.

Nay.

IT APPEARED each day his strength returned, and his leg troubled him less. When court day arrived, he left the bed and noticed the lessened pain almost to the point of no longer troubling. Even though it had been a week since their disagreement, he turned to look at the space in the bed that his wife should occupy.

Not there. The same as it had been since they'd had their disagreement a week ago. Stubborn lass.

They shared meals, discussed any issue she was having with the keep, but otherwise she avoided him. He groused at everyone who tried to speak with him until Conall threatened to flatten him if he didn't make things right with his wife.

It had felt good to knock the mon onto his arse, even if he grinned at him as he sat rubbing his chin.

With a groan at what he faced that day, he made his way over to the wash bowl. After washing and cleaning his teeth, he dressed, happy that he was able to do it without help since he doubted Ainslee would be willing to help him, although he could make it one of her wifely duties.

Christ's toes, the woman would drive him daft.

Then despite his frustration, he smiled at her staring up at him from the bed the night of their argument, defying him, even though he appeared as threatening as he kenned he did. Spirited lass. Just what he dinna want when he'd selected Elsbeth.

After living for months with the two sisters, he would be dishonest enough to need a confessor if he pretended Elsbeth would have suited him better. Aye, his life would be easier, but he had a feeling he would soon forget he even had a wife, so quiet and biddable the lass was.

That no longer appealed to him.

There was no time this morn to reflect on it, but mayhaps he would consider Ainslee's thoughts about her place in the castle. And their marriage.

With a healthy gait, he left his room and made his way downstairs. Ainslee was nowhere in sight when he entered the great hall. He had much to prepare for, so he had no desire to wander the castle searching for her.

One of the servants came into the great hall. "Good morn, my laird. Are ye ready to break yer fast?"

"Aye. Do ye ken where your lady is?"

"Nay. I haven't seen her yet this morn."

He grunted. "When ye see her, please ask her to join me."

Before he took a sip of his ale, Conall wandered into the room, taking a seat across from him. "Ye look like hell, brother."

"And good morn to ye as well."

Conall reached for a cup of ale and studied his brother over the rim. "Since I heard Ainslee moving about in the room next to me, I assume yer still at odds with the lass?"

"Nay. I told ye before, I dinna wish to tell ye anything about my wife. 'Tis none of yer business."

Conall shrugged. "If ye want my advice, ye can always

ask. I have a lot more experience with the lasses than ye do." The obnoxious mon winked at him.

Haydon slammed his fist down on the table. " I need no one's advice about my wife." He pointed at his brother. "And ye have way too much experience with the lasses, and one day 'twill catch up with you."

His idiot brother merely smiled and continued to eat the porridge set down in front of them by the servant.

18

Ainslee was miserable. She hated sleeping away from her husband but refused to admit defeat and become the mousy wee wife he wanted. Or he thought he wanted. Even though she had suspected when she offered to switch places with her sister that she suited the arrogant oaf much more than Elsbeth, living with him had proved her right.

Her sister still refused to look Haydon in the eyes when he spoke with her and was all too glad to leave his presence whenever she could. Ainslee shook her head. What a sorry marriage that would have been.

Was hers any better? Aye, she stood up to him, but where had it gotten her? Cold and lonely in her bed each night.

Blast the mon. At one time she would have thought it dinna matter, but she'd grown used to having him next to her all night, curled up to his warm body. Having him make love to her, offering pleasure she had never dreamed of.

And worst of all, she'd fallen in love with the brute.

Since 'twas court day, she intended to be present. No' at her husband's side, of course, but at least in the room so she could see how he ran the court.

She purposely dressed in her finest gown, spent a great deal of time brushing her hair until it shone, letting it fall down her back in a riot of dark red curls. She even bit her lips and pinched her cheeks before she entered the great hall.

Let her husband see what he was missing.

The room was filling up. Since it had been a while since the last court day, it would probably take all day to hear everyone's petitions. Of course, 'twould be a lighter load had her stubborn husband agreed to have help.

She made sure she walked slowly to one of the benches, swaying her hips and smiling at the men. Underneath her lowered eyelashes, she saw Haydon studying her as she made her way through the throng.

The possession, need, and desire in his eyes lifted her spirits. Apparently, he was suffering as well. Although the clod would ne'er admit it.

Just as she raised her eyelids, he quickly turned his head, obviously not wanting to be caught staring at her.

One more point for her side.

Despite her success in annoying her husband, she was appalled to see no other women in the room. Even all the petitioners were men. Did none of the women have issues to be settled? Most likely their husbands spoke for them. 'Twas a situation Ainslee was not happy with and would try her best to change.

Eventually Haydon stood and declared court open.

Conall stood in front of him and read the first name on the list.

Andrew Sutherland walked to the front of the room, his hands crushing his hat. With a great deal of waving of his arms and glaring at the mon sitting two rows back, he told the story of his neighbor and a stolen cow. Andrew claimed to have a final deal with the mon offering the animal for sale, but when he went to bring the coin to the mon and pick up the cow, he found his neighbor had already bought it. Andrew said the only way his neighbor kenned of the animal was through him.

He shook his fist. "He stole it!"

Haydon called the former owner of the cow and the mon who bought it to the front and began questioning them.

Three other cases had been settled when the door to the great hall opened and Patrick entered the room. Donal's father looked presentable for once and had a woman alongside him. A woman with a black eye.

He ambled up to Conall and after speaking with him, Conall wrote his name on the list of petitioners.

Donal!

The mon wanted his son returned to him. Nay. Nay. Nay. She would ne'er allow that. She quickly hurried from the room in search of the lad.

It didn't take her too long to find him. As usual, he was hanging around the kitchen. He grinned at her when she entered. "Good morn, my lady."

The bairn was well fed, happy, and like all wee lads, mischievous. There remained no evidence of the brutal life he'd led before Ainslee and Haydon rescued him from his da.

"Donal, do me a wee favor and go out to the garden and see if Lady Elsbeth has herbs ye can bring in."

He jumped from his seat, shoving the last piece of an oatcake into his mouth and raced to the door. She smiled. He was always in a hurry.

"What is it ye wish to speak with me about, my lady?" Jonet was no fool.

"May we step outside for a moment?" If this worked out for her, she dinna want anyone else in the keep to ken about it.

Jonet wiped her hands on her apron and followed Ainslee outside. "This is about the lad, isna it?"

"Aye." Ainslee placed her hands on her hips and regarded the woman who loved Donal like one of her own bairns. "Court is being held today."

Jonet nodded.

"Just now, Patrick entered the great hall, along with a woman I'd never seen before. The poor lass had a black eye."

Jonet sucked in a breath.

"Aye. I'm certain he will ask for the lad to be returned to him. I canna allow that."

"Nay. The poor lad is verra happy here."

Ainslee took a deep breath. "I am going to ask a favor of ye." She hesitated for a moment since she was asking the woman to go against her laird. "I want to bring Donal to yer house to stay for a while until I can convince my husband that the lad should not be returned."

The woman chewed her lip.

"I understand I am asking ye to take a chance doing this, but if we can keep the laird from asking if he is at yer house, ye won't have to lie to him. I plan to tell him I hid the lad and take the brunt of his anger."

"Are ye sure ye want to do this, my lady?"

"I have no choice. Ye ken what will happen to wee Donal if he goes back to his da. We'll ne'er see him alive again."

Jonet shook her head. "We canna have that." She raised her chin. "Aye. I will do it."

Ainslee hugged the cook, tears in her eyes. "Thank ye. I will pack the lad's things and bring him there now. I must take him right away since I want him well gone before court ends." She hesitated for a moment. " I assume yer daughter, Arabella, minds the little ones while yer here?"

"Aye. She is a fine one to watch them too. She doona take any nonsense from them. Donal will be fine with her."

Feeling quite relieved, Ainslee hurried to the nursery where Donal had been staying since his arrival. She packed his belongings and raced back down the stairs, anxious to get the lad away from the keep.

Donal had returned to the kitchen by the time she arrived. Jonet was speaking with him, and she assumed from the look on the lad's face, he kenned why he was being sent to Jonet's house.

"My lady, ye willna let me da take me?" The poor lad looked scared to death.

"Nay. That will ne'er happen. Ye can trust me, Donal. Ye will be safe. Now, 'tis time for us to go."

Not wanting to take a chance, Ainslee and Donal left through the kitchen door. They got as far as the gate when she realized they would be stopped if they left through the main entrance.

"Come, Donal, we must find another way out of the keep."

"I ken of one, my lady."

"Ye do?"

"Aye. When I want to leave the keep to explore, I go out a hole in the wall near where they put the baking oven."

Ainslee couldn't help but smile at the lad. However, she would speak with the head builder about the hole. Convenient for now, but unsafe for the clan.

Luckily, the hole was big enough for the two of them to fit through. Taking the lad's hand after they climbed out, they began to run toward the village where Jonet's house was.

Within an hour they arrived, somewhat out of breath. But they'd done it. The lad was safe. She explained the situation to Arabella who looked with sympathy at Donal. "Ye will be safe here, Donal. I heard a lot about ye from my mam." She wagged her finger at him. "But ye must behave yerself. Like the other wee ones."

Donal nodded. "Aye, Arabella. I will no' give ye any trouble."

With a final hug and kiss upon his head, Ainslee left Donal and made her way back to the castle. She fully intended to crawl back through the hole so no one would ken she'd left the castle at all.

* * *

HAYDON WATCHED as Ainslee left the great hall. She seemed in a hurry, but he'd been busy dispatching justice between a mon and his daughter. The lass in question had run off to be with her young mon, and once the da had caught up with her, 'twas too late. The damage had been done.

Haydon looked at the tear-streaked face of the lass. "What is yer name, lass?"

"Elene, my laird."

"Why did she feel the need to run off?" Haydon asked her da, Douglas Sutherland, a far-removed cousin of his.

The mon glared at the lad. "The lad is no good."

Haydon leaned back, his fingers tapping on the armrest of his chair. "Why do ye say that?"

"Isna the fact that he allowed her to come to him behind my back enough?"

It appeared they were going in circles. Haydon looked at the lad. "What is yer name?"

"Hamish Sutherland, my laird." He cast loving glances at Douglas's daughter who smiled back at him, a slight blush on her face.

"Do ye wish to marry the lass?"

"Aye, my laird. I asked permission from her da many times, but he always said 'nay.'"

Haydon turned his attention back to Douglas. "What say ye? Why did ye turn the lad down? And doona tell me because he visited yer daughter behind yer back. It seems to me he wouldna done that if ye hadn't refused to let him see her."

"I want better for my lass. Someone with land and money."

Haydon frowned. "Did ye have someone in mind?"

"Nay. But I've been looking."

A soft chuckle arose from the crowd.

"Well, it seems to me ye need to look no further. The

lad wants to marry the lass, and she appears to want to marry him. The best thing for a happy marriage is love, which it appears has struck these two."

He stopped as though a bolt of lightning had struck him. *The best thing for a happy marriage is love.*

Why the devil had he said that? He sounded like a besotted fool himself. From the corner of his eye, he saw Conall break out into a huge grin.

He would pummel him later.

"I suggest ye visit with the priest and get these two married." He looked at Hamish. "Do ye have a house, lad?"

"Nay. I live with my mam and da, working their fields."

Haydon folded his hands on the table in front of him. "I will send some of my men to help ye build a small house. Close enough to your da's land so ye can continue to help him and take some of the profits until ye can get yer own fields producing."

The lad let out a deep breath of relief. "Thank ye, my laird." He placed his arm around the lass's shoulders. "I will take good care of her."

"Ye better, or ye will answer to me."

Elene snuggled against Hamish's chest and wrapped her arms around his waist.

A cloud of depression descended on Haydon. Since Hamish was merely a farmer, there would be no reason for this young couple to fight about who was in charge, and who would make the decisions.

Hamish would provide for her and whatever bairns came along. Elene would see that everyone was warm, comfortable, and well fed. A simple life. But unfortunately, not his.

There were three more cases to dispense with before

Patrick stood before him. "What brings ye here today, Patrick?"

He had to admit the mon did look presentable. Certainly better than when they'd taken Donal from him.

He shuffled back and forth, moving his body from one foot to the other. "I want my lad back."

Haydon studied him for a moment. "The lad is doing quite well here. While I believe a bairn should be with his da and mam, from what we saw a few weeks ago, ye weren't doing right by the lad. What's changed?"

Patrick reached behind him and pulled a woman up next to him. "I got married. The lad will have a mam now."

The woman looked tired, worn, and sported a black eye. Haydon looked at her. "What is yer name, lass?"

"Rinalda, my laird." Her voice was soft and low. She glanced at him briefly and then stared at the floor.

"And how did ye hurt yer eye?"

She looked over at Patrick who gave a curt nod.

"I fell and hit the table," she mumbled.

He believed that as much as he believed a unicorn would soon appear in the great hall. However, it had to seem as though he was considering the idea since there were others watching who kenned nothing about Donal and Patrick and expected the laird to be fair.

Turning to Conall, he said, "Find the lad. Bring him here."

There were only two other petitioners to be heard, so Haydon asked Patrick and Rinalda to wait until Donal arrived while he continued with his cases.

They were both simple arguments over thievery on both sides. Just as he finished with the last one, Conall entered the great hall.

Alone.

"Where's the lad?" Haydon asked.

Conall shrugged. "I've searched the entire keep. No one kens."

Haydon tapped his finger on the table. Patrick arrived, Ainslee disappeared, and now Donal was missing. "Have ye seen yer lady?"

"Aye. She's in the kitchen."

He had no intention of questioning his wife in front of those left in the great hall. He looked over at Patrick. "We will need to continue this another time."

The man's temper almost got the best of him which made Haydon wonder how 'reformed' the mon was. "I will notify ye when ye need to appear again."

Patrick stomped out of the room, his wife trailing behind him. Not looking forward to the following confrontation with his wife, Haydon left the great hall.

Ainslee was sitting at one of the worktables cutting up meat. From the way her hand shook 'twas a wonder she hadn't cut off a finger or two. "My lady."

She looked up. "Aye, my laird?"

"I would have a word with ye in our bedchamber."

Slowly, she placed the knife on the table and followed him out of the kitchen and up the stairs to their bedchamber. He held the door open, and she stepped through. Ainslee immediately moved to the hearth and took a seat in front of the fire.

He joined her in the chair opposite. "Where is Donal?"

"I'm afraid I cannot say."

Haydon hopped up and leaned against the fireplace mantle. "I ordered the lad to be brought to the great hall, and it seems he cannot be found anywhere in the castle."

She shrugged.

He walked to her chair and placed his hands on the arms, leaning verra close to her face. "Where. Is. The. Lad?"

She shook her head.

"I will try this one more time. I am yer laird. I am asking ye a question. I expect ye to answer."

He was taken off guard when she placed her hands on his chest and shoved him back. He stumbled, and she jumped up. "I willna tell ye where the lad is so ye can send him back to that cursed da of his."

Haydon's jaw dropped. "Think ye I would send him back to Patrick?" His voice rose enough to alert the rest of the keep of their argument. "Ye trust me so little, wife? The mon is not fit to raise a pig, let alone a bairn."

"Then why did ye want him brought to the great hall?"

He slammed his fist down on the table. "'Tis no' yer concern. I make the decisions in court, as well as all others."

Ainslee collapsed onto the chair, shaking her head slowly. "'Tis not going to work, Haydon." She looked up at him with a great sadness in her eyes. "I canno' be married to a mon who respects me so little. A husband who wants no more from me than what ye expect."

He turned and strode across the room, looking out the window, studying the peaceful surroundings of early spring. He loved this time of the year, but now he was too miserable to appreciate it.

Or anything else.

He heard her climb to her feet and walk to the bedchamber door. "I will continue to stay in the other bedchamber until the bairn is born. Then I will travel to my da's castle."

Haydon whipped around. "Nay. Ye will not take my son from me."

She offered a soft laugh. "Could verra well be a daughter, my laird."

"It doona matter. Ye will not take my bairn from Dornoch."

"Ach, Haydon. Dinna ye see ye trust me no more than ye say I doona trust ye? Think ye I would take the bairn away from ye forever? Have a bairn of mine ne'er ken his da? Nay. I mean to take a trip to visit my da. I need time away to think."

She opened the door and stepped through. When the silence continued, she turned to him and said, "We could have had so much more."

Haydon collapsed on the bed, his heart breaking. Aye. Breaking. Because he loved the lass. Wanted her forever by his side. But she wanted things from him he wasn't familiar with. His da ruled the castle without interference from his wife. 'Twas the only example Haydon had ever seen. He'd always assumed his life would be the same.

Except were that true, would he have agreed to the bride switch many weeks ago at the wedding? He had the chance to stop the ceremony, yet he hadn't.

He also had to get away and think.

19

*H*aydon barreled out of the keep and strode to the stable. Conall's voice called to him, but he kept going. He wasn't in the mood for Conall's 'advice'. He created this problem with his wife, and he needed to find a way to fix it.

His way.

Aye, and how much success had ye had doing things yer way?

He tacked Demon himself and rode as fast as he could away from the castle. He kenned exactly where he was headed. When he and Conall were growing up, they spent time in an abandoned cottage in the woods not too far from the castle. They'd stocked it with firewood and dried meat. When they grew older and still felt the need to get away occasionally, they added whisky to the larder.

'Twas just what he needed to sort it all out.

. . .

He was feeling the results of his first few swigs of the whisky bottle when the door to the cottage slammed open and Conall stepped through.

Haydon growled. "I dinna need to hear yer 'advice'. Ye can leave now."

Almost as if his brother had read his mind, he said, "And how much success have ye had without my advice?" He looked at the bottle and glass Haydon held in his hand. "Care to share that, brother?"

Haydon waved the bottle around. "Get yer own."

Conall strolled to Haydon and slid the bottle from his hand. "'Tis mine. I put the last couple of bottles in here."

They sat in uncomfortable silence for about five minutes when Conall began his attack. "Ye are an arse."

"Watch yer mouth, brother. I am yer laird."

"Aye. A laird's arse."

Too weary to get up and punch the mon in the face, Haydon merely took another sip of whisky. "Ye are banned from the clan. Ye can pack up yer things and leave anytime."

The fool mon laughed. "That's yer problem, brother. Anything that displeases ye, that challenges ye, ye push away."

When Haydon said nothing, Conall continued. "Ye have the best wife ever, and ye are trying yer damnedest to change her. To make her into a wife ye wouldna be able to stand for more than a month."

"If ye remember, brother, Ainslee was not my choice."

Conall's brows rose. "Aye? Think ye can fool me? 'Twould have been no difficulty whatsoever to call a halt to the wedding when ye discovered the lasses' deviousness. Yet ye went ahead with the ceremony."

Haydon downed the rest of his drink. "'Twould have been too embarrassing for her da."

Conall threw his head back and laughed. "And is that the story ye've been telling yerself? That 'twas to avoid embarrassment that led ye to continue with the wedding?"

"Isno' there somewhere else you need to be?"

Conall stood and walked over to his brother and refilled his glass. "Nay. The best place I can be right now is here making yer hard head listen to some sense."

Haydon closed his eyes and rested his head against the back of the chair. "I hope ye dinna mind if I take a nap while ye prattle on."

"Let me ask ye a question. Are ye truly happy with the way things are between ye and Ainslee?"

Haydon saw no reason to answer. 'Twas obvious to probably everyone in the castle that he and Ainslee were sleeping apart. That dinna make for a happy marriage, for certain.

"Ye ken I always looked up to ye. As a brother, a warrior, and a laird. I thought ye could do no wrong. That ye were smart and made the best decisions."

Haydon opened one eye. "Why do I think all this praise is about to come tumbling down?"

"Ye love her."

The words just hung there in the air. He'd no intention of falling in love with his wife. Love caused one to do strange things.

Like run to the nearest retreat and drink yerself into a stupor?

A laird had to be strong and decisive, he couldna be following his wife around like a lovesick fool.

He hadn't realized he'd said those things out loud until

Conall said, "Ye are an even bigger fool than I thought. Mayhaps there is no saving ye."

Haydon sat forward, resting his arms on his thighs. "Da ne'er depended on mam to make decisions. He ran the court himself as well as the clan. This idea of being partners is confusing."

"Ach. Now yer making sense. 'Tis confusing, but 'twas not what da had wanted."

Haydon placed his cup on the table. "What are ye talking about?"

"Ye were off fostering for years while Grandda ran the keep and then Da, when Grandda died."

"Aye."

"Grandda always had Grandmam by his side during court. He also asked her advice on many things."

Haydon shook his head at such nonsense. "Nay. If that is so, then why didn't Da do the same with Mam?"

Conall shrugged. "He wanted to. But Mam came from a clan that felt the same as ye do. The laird ran everything related to the clan, made all the decisions, and the women dinna do more than produce bairns and make the mon comfortable. She dinna want to do any more than that."

Haydon felt as though someone had slapped him in the face with a wet cloth. "But I spent time with Da before he died when I returned from fostering. He ne'er said anything like that."

"Mayhaps he had given up on it by then. Ye ken he only ran the clan for a few years before he was killed in battle, and it all passed to ye. With the various wars going on, he was absent quite a bit. I oftentimes thought a lot of his offering to take up his sword was due to missing

Mam." He hesitated for a moment. "They had a love match, ye ken."

Haydon could say he thought they did, but since he'd spent so much time away from home when he was growing up, he dinna see a lot of what passed between them. He just remembered his da's sadness when Mam died from a chill she'd caught after being caught in the rain.

"Ye ken, loving yer wife is a rare thing, especially among those who are expected to marry for alliances. Ye are a lucky mon, my laird. Doona throw it all away because yer stubborn." With those words, Conall downed the rest of his drink and left the cottage.

Haydon stayed behind no more than five minutes after he heard Conall's horse galloping away. 'Twas a sad day in his life that he was considering heeding his brother's advice.

He *was* a lucky mon. And he did marry the right sister. He'd kenned that from the day of the wedding. He loved Ainslee, and he kenned in his heart she loved him as well. Allowing them to be partners could change their lives. Based on what he did next, they could have a wonderful life, or they could be miserable for years.

Since he was never fond of misery, he left the cottage, jumped on Demon, and headed home. To his wife. The woman he dinna wish to spend any more time away from. He'd gather her into his arms, sweep her up to their bedchamber, and show her how much he loved her.

Then they would have a serious talk and they would work out a partnership. He tried no' to wince at the word, but what was at stake was too important for stubbornness.

* * *

AINSLEE WANDERED THE KEEP, going from room to room, but finding nothing to occupy her time. The rooms had all been cleaned and restored, and the servants were doing a fine job of keeping everything tidy.

The kitchen, as usual, was running smoothly and didn't need her assistance. No one needed her. Especially her husband.

With a deep sigh, she strolled past Haydon's solar and came to an abrupt stop. The door was partially opened. She pushed it farther and took in a deep breath.

A mon she'd never seen before was rifling through the drawers in Haydon's desk. Without thinking, she said, "What are you doing?"

He jerked at the sound of her voice and looked up. Before she could react, he flew across the room, slammed the door closed, then wrapped his arm around her neck. He squeezed slightly, but enough to cut off some of her air. She reached up and tried to pry his arm off her. "I can't breathe."

He moved his other hand up, waving a dagger in her face. "Ye won't be breathing at all anymore if ye make one sound."

She nodded, black dots beginning to form in her eyes. Just as she thought she would crumble to the floor, he released her neck, but grabbed her upper arm, dragging her across the room. He tossed her into the chair behind Haydon's desk and ran his fingers through his hair. "What am I to do with ye?"

Since she dinna believe he would like her answer, she kept quiet, but looked around the room to see if there was something she could grab as a weapon. Talking might help while she gave herself time to think. "What are ye doing in here?"

He chuckled. "Ye should ken what I'm doing in here, ye spent enough time telling everyone to stay out of this room. Important papers ye said. Foolish woman. Like most, ye talk too much."

"I ne'er seen ye before."

He took the papers he'd found in the desk—as they'd planned—and shoved them into a leather satchel draped across his body. "Nay. A few of yer lasses here are the 'friendly' sort. If a mon talks sweet to them, they're ready to lift their skirts. They like to chatter away when we're done, if ye get my drift. It amazes me what a lass will say when she thinks yer no' paying attention."

He placed his hands on his hips and studied her. "I had no intention of killing anyone. I just wanted to get these papers and collect my money. Off to the New World, I am." He blew out a breath, then walked around the desk and pulled her up.

"We're going for a wee stroll." He wrapped his arm round her waist, placing the dagger against her ribs. "If ye make any noise, I will go against my dislike for killing and leave ye to bleed to death. Otherwise, we'll go for a short ride and then I'll dump ye where ye can walk back."

They left the room and walked briskly to the back door of the keep. Ainslee was amazed that the few people they saw merely nodded at them. They stepped outside and to her surprise, the mon brought her to the hole in the wall she and Donal had escaped through earlier.

He lowered her head and pushed her from behind. "Go on, lass." She thought about running or calling out before he made it through the hole, but he'd most likely catch her before anyone could help, and she kenned in her heart he would slit her throat rather than be caught.

He grasped her elbow, the dagger still pressed against her, and hurried them to a horse standing in a clump of trees. He tossed her up onto the horse's back and before her bottom even landed, he was behind her, his arm wrapped tightly around her waist. With a flick of his wrist, the horse took off.

* * *

HAYDON PUSHED Demon to go faster as he made his way from the cottage. He felt as though he were flying, and not just because of the horse's speed. The cloud of depression that had followed him since his wife announced she would remain in a different bedchamber until the bairn was born had lifted.

He loved her and wanted her to be his partner. He had no idea what that meant, but he trusted Ainslee enough to ken she would no' take advantage. She merely wanted to be a part of his life, and he was tired of pushing her away.

He would do and say whatever it took to convince her that their marriage could be the kind she'd always dreamed of.

Racing into the keep, he was stopped by old Broderick coming out the main door. "Aye, glad I caught ye, my laird. I've been looking for ye everywhere."

Haydon's stomach sank. He could tell by the look in old Broderick's eyes that his news was not good news. "What is it?"

"Just about half past an hour ago yer lady raced away

with a mon I'd ne'er seen before. Both of them on a horse I ne'er seen before, either." He waved his finger in Haydon's face. "I'll tell ye this much, my laird. That lass was not leaving of her own free will."

"Which way did they go?"

Old Broderick pointed south. "That way."

"Thank ye." Haydon returned to the stable. Luckily Angus had not removed the animal's tack, so it took no time at all to hop back onto the horse and head in the direction old Broderick had pointed.

What the devil was going on? His first thought was that Ainslee had left him, but then he realized she wouldna do it that way. She was much too courageous and forthright. Were she to leave him, she would make sure he kenned it, and why, and how, and when.

Loudly.

He smiled. Aye, his Ainslee was no wilting flower.

But that made it more dangerous. Who had her, and for what purpose? Was it somehow tied into their search for the traitor? Had she stumbled upon him while Haydon was at the cottage feeling sorry for himself?

His heart thundered along with the horse's hooves. If anything happened to her, he would never recover. Why had it taken this long to realize how much she meant to him? How much he needed her in his life? Conall was right about one thing. He was an arse.

Not even sure he was going along the same route they'd taken, he prayed for the first time in a long while. No sooner had the heartfelt words left his mouth than he spotted a figure on the pathway ahead of him coming in his direction. Not on a horse, but walking. With a limp.

As he drew nearer, he began to suspect it was a

woman. On foot. Alone. In dangerous territory. God's bones, it was Ainslee!

He pushed Demon even harder and circled around, scooped Ainslee into his arms and crushed her against him. "Ach, lass. Ye had me scared to death."

To his surprise and dismay, his courageous wife burst into tears.

He dinna feel as though they were safe, even though they were on Sutherland land. Outlaws were always around and even the occasional British soldier who'd decamped and wandered the woods.

Rather than stop to comfort her, he kissed the top of her head. "Hang on, *mo ghràdh*, I'll have ye home in no time."

By the time they reached inside the castle gates, Ainslee had stopped crying and sat slumped against him. "Ainslee?"

She raised her head. "Aye?"

"Come." He jumped down and gripped her waist. Once her feet hit the ground, she cried out and collapsed against him. He lifted her into his arms and headed to the keep. On the way he shouted at one of the men. "Have the healer come to my bedchamber."

Taking the stairs two at a time, he headed toward their bedchamber, kicking the door open. With a few strides he reached the bed and gently placed her on it. He smoothed the hair back from her forehead. "What happened to yer leg, *mo chridhe?*

"'Tis my foot. When he tossed me from the horse, I twisted my ankle."

"I ken ye have a long story to tell me, but right now I want the healer to see to yer foot. Then ye will soak in a warm bath, and we'll have our evening meal sent up here. Then we shall talk." He stopped to re-think. "What I mean, lass, is if ye wish to, we shall talk."

Ainslee nodded and closed her eyes, a slight smile on her face.

Dorathia Sutherland, the clan healer, rushed into the room, clearly out of breath, Elsbeth following close behind her.

"What happened, my laird?" 'Twas the first time his sister by marriage looked him in the eye.

"I'm not sure yet, but I ken Ainslee hurt her foot. That's all I'm concerned with now." He stepped back as Dorathia leaned over Ainslee.

"Tell me how ye hurt yer foot."

Ainslee repeated the story she'd told Haydon. Nothing more. He dinna care because he wanted her feeling better.

Haydon hovered over Ainslee until Dorathia had to ask him to step back so she could work. But there was a bright smile on her face when she did so.

Refusing to move too far from her, he took his wife's hand and squeezed it. "Elsbeth, please arrange to have a bath set up for Ainslee when Dorathia is finished with her."

He watched every move Dorathia made and winced when Ainslee winced. Sucked in a breath when Ainslee sucked in breath. Frowned when Ainslee frowned.

Now that she was safe and sound in their bedchamber, he was able to relax. She hadn't ordered him from the room, so mayhaps there was a chance for him to make things up to her.

Three bulky men toted in a wooden bathtub, followed by several maids carrying buckets of steaming water, and one or two of cold water to cool the temperature.

Dorathia began to pack up her satchel. "My lady, ye only have a sprain, but a bad one. I suggest ye remain off yer feet for a least three days. If my laird can fashion ye a cane, ye can use that once ye've rested enough."

"I shall make one first thing in the morn." Haydon continued to hold her hand, rubbing his thumb over her knuckles.

She picked up the satchel. "Be sure to keep the bandage tightly wrapped around yer foot and ankle. That will help with the healing." She looked over her shoulder at the tub. "Ye can enjoy a bath but remember to keep yer foot out of the water."

"Aye. I'll see that she is well taken care of, Dorathia."

Elsbeth returned, but wanting time along with his wife, he asked her to go back to the kitchen and ask Jonet to send up their evening meal in about an hour.

"And include a jug of wine with it."

Apparently aware of the fact that Haydon wanted her gone, Elsbeth grinned and left the room, not far behind the healer.

"Do ye feel up to a bath, lass?"

"Aye. I feel dirty after being handled by that mon."

His muscles clenched, and he felt the need to punch something. 'Tis all right, he told himself. She dinna look as though she had been harmed in any way outside of her ankle. Her clothes were not torn or stained. When she was ready, she would tell him what happened. He needed to be patient.

"Come, I will help ye undress." He pulled her into a sitting position and helped her out of her clothes. He wrapped his arm around her, and she began to hobble along. With one quick move, he swept her into his arms and carried her to the tub.

"Be careful of my foot," she said as he lowered her into the water. She sighed with contentment as she leaned her head back.

"I'll wash yer hair for ye."

* * *

AINSLEE MOANED with pleasure as Haydon rubbed her head with the lavender-scented soap. 'Twas a luxury to have someone wash her hair, and the fact that her arrogant oaf of a braw husband was doing so made it even better.

She was not all that surprised when she saw Haydon racing down the road toward her, never doubting that he would come for her. She was just grateful he'd found her before it grew dark.

What she'd noticed from the time he scooped her up and plopped her in front of him on the horse was a difference in his attitude. He seemed softer, more patient, and dare she use the word? Loving.

Could it be he'd had a change of heart? She kenned he wouldn't be satisfied until she told him the entire tale. Which she intended to do but wanted to feel safe and cared for before she recalled the horror.

After rinsing her hair and helping her from the bathtub, he helped dry her off. "I'll help ye to one of the chairs by the fire. Ye shall be warm enough."

Haydon went around picking up the linens and her

clothing from the floor like a lady's maid. She couldn't help laughing but kept it to herself.

A knock on the door drew their attention. Haydon opened it and allowed one of the kitchen maids to carry in a tray. She placed it on the table between the two chairs in front of the fire. Ainslee breathed in the wonderful aroma of roasted pig, vegetables, warm bread, butter, and apple pasties.

They did a fine job of devouring the food as well as draining the jug of wine. Ainslee leaned back and rubbed her tummy. "I guess I can give myself the excuse of eating for two now."

Haydon placed his cup carefully on the table. He shifted off his chair and lowered his large body to his knees in front of her. He took both her hands in his. "I'm an arse."

"Aye."

He smiled. "Ye could have disagreed."

"Nay."

"I need ye, Ainslee. More than I realized. 'Twasn't until ye said ye were leaving after the bairn is born that made me admit what I'd been pushing aside for a long time."

She tilted her head and studied him. "What is that, my laird?"

"Nay. Not yer laird but yer husband. Yer lover." He kissed her knuckles. "Yer partner."

Tears sprang to her eyes. "Partner?"

He nodded. "Aye. I need ye beside me, lass. I need yer help, guidance, and advice. I canno' do it alone. I dinna want to do it alone. I love ye, wife. More than I ever thought I would."

"Ach, husband. I love ye, too. Even though yer an arrogant oaf and an arse."

"That bad, eh?"

"Aye. That bad, but I love ye anyway." She reached out and stroked his strong jaw, loving the scratch of his bristles on her fingers.

He kissed her hand again. "Someone once said *the best thing for a happy marriage is love.*

"A wise mon for sure."

He tugged her so she landed on his lap. "I agree. What say ye we retreat to that comfortable bed, and I'll show ye how much I love ye, lass?"

She kissed his chin. "Doona ye want to ken what happened to me?"

"Aye. But make it quick since I want to love ye. Yer here with me, safe and sound. 'Tis all that matters."

After a quick retelling of how she stumbled upon the unknown mon in the solar, his dragging her off, and her being tossed from the horse and hurting her ankle, Haydon said, "Then our plan worked. 'Tis relieved I am that 'twas not one of our own that betrayed us. As ye say, he is headed to the New World after passing along the information we left for him. I canno' track the mon down and kill him for hurting my wife, so instead let me show ye how much I love ye."

Ainslee smirked. "And as yer partner, I will show you how much I love *ye.*"

EPILOGUE

Six years later
Dornoch Castle

"I dinna care if ye prefer to be outside climbing trees, Susanna, 'tis court day and ye need to learn how to advise yer husband when the day comes."

The five-year-old rolled her eyes at her da. "I doona want a husband. How many times do I need to tell ye? And I doona want to be inside listening to complaints. Court day is no' interesting."

Haydon, Laird of Sutherland, looked at his daughter with her deep green eyes and dark red hair just like her mam and smiled. "Doona let yer mam hear ye say that."

Susanna leaned in closer to her da's ear and patted his cheek. "'Tis our secret, then."

Aye, the lass had much of her mam in her. And like her mam, had him twisted around her little finger.

Just then Ainslee entered the great hall as the petitioners continued to arrive and give their names to Donal, the lad who was now their son and loved to work alongside his da. He diligently wrote the names at each court session but continued to harass Haydon to be allowed to start his warrior training. He was certainly getting old enough.

Ainslee took the seat alongside her husband, attempting to settle their son, Alasdair on her quickly disappearing lap. Their next bairn was due to arrive within another month. The lad wiggled and held his arms out to Haydon.

"Ach, the lad wants nothing to do with his mam when his da is around," Ainslee said.

Haydon took the bairn in his arms as he looked out over the crowd, noting the scattering of women. Ainslee had been working hard to get the clanswomen more involved in the clan. The younger ones accepted the change easier than the older, more set-in-their-ways women.

Their agreement to be partners had worked so well, Haydon felt as though he would never be able to manage the clan without his wife's help.

Aye, she was producing bairns and running the keep, but she also made him feel complete. 'Twas a smart move he'd made, offering for Ainslee back at Lochwood Tower all those years ago. A verra smart move, indeed.

Did you like this story? Please consider leaving a review on either Goodreads or the place where you bought it. Long or short, your review will help other readers discover new authors and make purchasing decisions!

I hope you had fun reading Ainslee and Haydon's love story. Want more Highlander romance? Look for the next book in the series, *To Marry a Highlander*.

He didn't mean for them to get caught...

Conall Sutherland, younger brother and right-hand man to Haydon, the laird of the Sutherland Clan, is happy with his life. Or was until recently. He'd never felt the pull of marriage, since he enjoys the company of the wenches who offer him room in their beds. Lately, however, things just don't seem right.

Maura Mac Ewan, Conall's distant cousin, has always had a fancy for him, but aware of his reputation with the lasses, she never encouraged him, fearing a broken heart. When the two are caught alone, in the dark, in each other's arms, it doesn't matter that it was innocent. Her father and brothers give them no choice.

Marriage.

Maura's hope for wedded bliss wavers when the many lasses at the keep who had spent time in her new husband's bed begin to harass her and cause her trouble. They try their best to make her miserable, flirting openly with Conall. Can she be certain that her husband has given up his libertine ways? Or is she doomed to spend her life with a man she can never trust?

Then things get worse...

Click here for more information:
https://calliehutton.com/the-sutherlands-of-dornoch/

* * *

You can find a list of all my books on my website: http://calliehutton.com/books/

ABOUT THE AUTHOR

Receive a free book and stay up to date with new releases and sales!
http://calliehutton.com/newsletter/

USA Today bestselling author, Callie Hutton, has penned more than 55 historical romance and cozy mystery books. She lives in Oklahoma with her very close and lively family, which includes her twin grandsons, affectionately known as "The Twinadoes."

Callie loves to hear from readers. Contact her directly at calliehutton11@gmail.com or find her online at www.calliehutton.com.

Connect with her on Facebook, Twitter, and Goodreads.

Follow her on BookBub to receive notice of new releases, preorders, and special promotions.

Praise for books by Callie Hutton

A Study in Murder

"This book is a delight!...*A Study in Murder* has clear echoes of Jane Austen, Agatha Christie, and of course, Sherlock Holmes. You will love this book." —William Bernhardt, author of *The Last Chance Lawyer*

"A one-of-a-kind new series that's packed with surprises." —Mary Ellen Hughes, National bestselling author of *A Curio Killing*.

"[A] lively and entertaining mystery...I predict a long run for this smart series." —Victoria Abbott, award-winning author of The Book Collector Mysteries

"With a breezy style and alluring, low-keyed humor, Hutton crafts a charming mystery with a delightful, irrepressible sleuth." —Madeline Hunter, *New York Times* bestselling author of *Never Deny a Duke*

The Elusive Wife

"I loved this book and you will too. Jason is a hottie & Oliva is the kind of woman we'd all want as a friend. Read it!" —Cocktails and Books

"In my experience I've had a few hits but more misses

with historical romance so I was really pleasantly surprised to be hooked from the start by obviously good writing." —Book Chick City

"The historic elements and sensory details of each scene make the story come to life, and certainly helps immerse the reader in the world that Olivia and Jason share." —The Romance Reviews

"You will not want to miss *The Elusive Wife*." —My Book Addiction

"…it was a well written plot and the characters were likeable." —Night Owl Reviews

A Run for Love

"An exciting, heart-warming Western love story!" —*New York Times* bestselling author Georgina Gentry

"I loved this book!!! I read the BEST historical romance last night…It's called *A Run For Love*." —*New York Times* bestselling author Sharon Sala

"This is my first Callie Hutton story, but it certainly won't be my last." —The Romance Reviews

An Angel in the Mail

"…a warm fuzzy sensuous read. I didn't put it down until I was done." —Sizzling Hot Reviews

Visit www.calliehutton.com for more information.